SKAC

G R E Y

D A W N

GREY DAWN

A Tale of Abolition and Union

NYRI A. BAKKALIAN

BALANCE OF SEVEN

Dallas

For information, contact:
Balance of Seven, www.balanceofseven.com
Publisher: dyfreeman@balanceofseven.com
Managing Editor: dtinker@balanceofseven.com

Cover Design by Lance Buckley, www.lancebuckley.com

Developmental Editing by Sarah Hines
Editing by D Tinker Editing, dtinker@balanceofseven.com

Japanese Language Consultant: Sarah Windsor
Korean Language Consultant: Minkyong Tinker

Publisher's Cataloging-in-Publication Data

Names: Bakkalian, Nyri A., author.
Title: Grey dawn : a tale of abolition and union / Nyri A. Bakkalian.
Description: Dallas, TX : Balance of Seven, 2020. | Summary: After months of
    pretending to be a man in the Union Army, a nineteenth-century lesbian
    falls through time to 2020. There, she meets a transgender veteran with
    the same name as the woman she left behind. This is a story of war,
    abolition, union, and connections that can last lifetimes.
Identifiers: LCCN 2020941040 | ISBN 9781947012059 (pbk.) | ISBN
    9781947012066 (ebook)
Subjects: LCSH: Gettysburg, Battle of, Gettysburg, Pa., 1863 -- Fiction. |
    United States -- History -- Civil War, 1861-1865 -- Fiction. | Lesbians --
    Fiction. | Transgender women -- Fiction. | Philadelphia (Pa.) -- Fiction. |
    BISAC: FICTION / Historical / Civil War Era. | FICTION / Romance
    / LGBT / General. | FICTION / Romance / Time Travel.
Classification: LCC PS3602.A3 G74 2020 (print) | PS3602.A3 (ebook) | DDC
    813 B35--dc23
LC record available at https://lccn.loc.gov/2020941040

24 23 22 21 20   1 2 3 4 5

To SL, because I made a promise;

as long as I live, I intend to keep it.

Cradle, well-cradle, well-cradle that measured who was taller.
I've grown taller, love, since I saw you last.

—Zeami Motokiyo, translated from *Izutsu* (*The Well-Cradle*)

History is written for the most part from the outside.

—Joshua Lawrence Chamberlain, *The Passing of the Armies*

CONTENTS

Acknowledgments	ix
One	1
Two	10
Three	29
Four	43
Five	62
Six	70
Seven	86
Eight	104
Nine	124
Ten	133
Eleven	142
Twelve	158
Thirteen	166
Fourteen	172
Fifteen	181
Sixteen	192
Seventeen	208
Epilogue	224

Illustrations   233

Acronyms   241

Want to Learn More about the Real History? 243

References   245

Bibliography   249

About the Author   251

ACKNOWLEDGMENTS

This book has had a long and perilous journey, but at last, it's in your hands. All I can say is, it's about time! But this was far from a solo endeavor.

Thank you to Kerry Lazarus, Gracie Jane Gollinger, Grace Dordevic, Ann E. Jenks, Joseph Davis, Sevag Bakalian, Sarah Kendall, Alan Cameron Caum, Sara Campbell-Szymanski, Michael T. Wells, Joe Kassabian, Beverly G. Gollinger, Shannon Massey, Gwendolyn Schmidt, Megan Linger, Meaghan Michel, Jonathan Bronson, Celosia Crane, Angry Staff Officer, Matt Palmquist, Vera Harriman, Emily Durham-Britton, Raffi Boujikanian, and many others for your beta reading, humor, gifts of journals and writing supplies, coffee, home cooking, expert knowledge on relevant topics, and shoulders to cry on when this project seemed insurmountable.

To the staff at Stenton, once the Logan estate, now a museum: thank you for a fascinating, thought-provoking tour that shed better light on the family's origins and complicated legacy. Your interest in this novel, willingness to indulge my questions, and permission to take reference photos in the mansion and on the grounds are humbling, and I will always be grateful. Thank you also for the chance to get to meet and pet Sallie, a most adorable feline curator and guardian.

Acknowledgments

Thank you also to Ynes Freeman, Tod Tinker, Andrea Coble, Sarah Hines, and everyone else at Balance of Seven for believing in this book, even when it was hard for me to do so.

Now, in the words of the great Alan Shepard, "Let's light this candle."

ONE

Excerpt from
Buford's Last Trooper: My War for Abolition and Union
Chloë Parker Stanton

We met—it was so long ago!—in 1858 during a raid. At least, that was the first we met.

We were an unlikely pair: she, born in a Fishtown tenement, the daughter of working-class Scotsmen; I, born at Cloughmore House, a daughter of privilege and power, with senators, judges, and men and women of letters in my pedigree and among my kin. Yet "we loved with a love that was more than love," Leigh Andrea Hunter and I, and in those dark days before the War to Suppress the Rebellion, she was my light.

When the war came, we parted, and I long feared it would be forever. In 1862, I enlisted in the Seventeenth Pennsylvania Volunteer Cavalry and went to be an instrument in the hands of an avenging Almighty, to draw by the sword a recompense for every blow of the slaver's infernal lash.

Three days after the Battle of Gettysburg, all changed when I was flung to the far future. Yet six months later, I would meet her again.

But I'm getting ahead of myself.

Back in 1858, it was the heyday of Bloody Kansas. John Brown and other Jayhawkers were doing the Almighty's work in driving slavers from what we then called the Kansas Territory. The Fugitive Slave Act was in force, and the travesty that was the Dred Scott v. Sandford decision had been but a year earlier. In short, we who stood on the ground of abolition knew it was time for action. Action! The men in Washington jawed and jawed and thumped their chests, but there were growing numbers of us who knew that we had to act, and we had to act swiftly and decisively. War was not here yet, but it was coming, and we wanted to be ready.

Philadelphia was, of course, a bastion of liberty, as it ever was. But the Mason-Dixon Line was not far at all, and more than a few prominent Southern families had homes here. There was many a day I saw bounty hunters and slaver posses on the streets of the city that bore me.

It was a life of comfort I'd had in Philadelphia, to be sure. Privilege as a daughter of the Stanton family had afforded me freedoms that few twenty-three-year-old women of my era possessed. We Stantons of Philadelphia have always prided ourselves on educating our children regardless of sex and on independence of action in the name of the good and right, even when it may not be politically expedient or popular.

The Stanton Act, which remains United States law, enshrines the stubborn tenacity that impelled my great-grandfather Senator George Stanton to take mediation into his own hands between the United States and France. *His* grandfather James Stanton was a politician—governor of Pennsylvania, no less—and a scientist, businessman, farmer, and autodidact praised by Linnaeus and by Franklin, the latter of whom was a most generous patron. The work of my great-grandmother Deborah Archer as a historian and antiquarian is also still remembered in the modern day.

In short, I was raised on my forefathers' books, I inherited my foremothers' sagacity, and like my great-grandfather, I knew how and did not fear to ride and shoot. Yet it was that same great-grandfather who had continued my ancestors' terrible tradition of slaveholding well into the 1780s. And so, acknowledging the terrible chapters of my family history while clinging to the good, I devoted myself to that quintessential spirit of the Society of Friends, the Quaker sense of justice and equality.

I tell you this that you might understand what was antecedent to my taking up arms, first on my own and later as a soldier of my country. And further, that you may appreciate what laid the path to my encountering Leigh that muggy night in spring 1858.

Some may tell you it was the white man who freed the black, but don't you believe it. A lot of us in that struggle were women, and many of those women were black. They had heeded the words of people like the esteemed Reverend Henry Highland Garnet, whose call to rebellion against slavery—after having himself fled bondage in Maryland—exhorted, "Let your motto be resistance! Resistance! RESISTANCE!"

They led the way. I merely used what I had and who I was to further aid their cause and thwart their oppressors. The Spirit moved me to act.

Unfortunately, my first foray into being a righteous weapon in the Spirit's hands did not go as smoothly as I had hoped.

It was after dark. Contrary to the wishful thinking of some in my time, the world did not go to sleep at night—

slave catchers included. It had been their aim, in that part of town, to seize people being moved under cover of night.

You must understand. When people talk as they do of a great "underground railroad," it is a tad misleading. It should not thereby be understood that we had some manner of corporate structure, that it were a single entity with one leader or commander. What I knew was a movement, organic, without a single leader or commander—just everyday people like you and I, with the black people themselves leading the way and the Spirit moving them to act.

I'd heard much talk about abolition over the years. I'd even seen no less than Frederick Douglass himself once speak at Germantown Friends Meeting. But there was no appreciable measure of action on the part of those with the most political power. They seemed more invested in maintaining the status quo than in doing what was right. And at long last, some of us cried "Enough!" and stood up to the slavers by force in Kansas, though others had long preceded them.

And in those days of Bleeding Kansas, there were some of us in Philadelphia, too, who were acting in concert with others, near and far.

This is how it was that that night in Fishtown found me out in the open night air, a revolver under my cloak and my heart in my throat. When I think back on it, I'm not sure I knew quite what I was doing yet. At home, my mother was none the wiser. She'd long since given up any real effort at taming me, though she still spoke often of finding me a husband. At night, she tended to let me be.

I'd heard tell at the meetinghouse that some fugitives sheltering in Fishtown on their way to British North America were going to be moved thenceforward to New York.

I'd also heard that more than one posse sent up from Virginia were active nearby and hunting.

So I acted.

It's funny. Back then, I don't know which would've been more illegal: that I was a woman armed, that I was a woman wearing pants, or that I was a woman acting against the provisions of the Fugitive Slave Act of 1850. I knew how to ride and how to shoot, sure, but I'd learned those on the grounds at Cloughmore and had never had occasion to call on those skills otherwise. All I knew was that I had to *do* something and that, as Lucretia Mott said, "I am no advocate of passivity. Quakerism, as I understand it, does not mean quietism."

What I'd like to say is that I succeeded and single-handedly killed or drove off a dozen men. What actually happened was not nearly that successful or heroic. But it was important, nonetheless, and even life changing.

I made it without interruption, to be sure. I was nearly to the riverfront, dismounting in an alley to tie up my horse, when I *heard* them. Benjamin Franklin described mobs the best: they have "heads enough but no brains." There weren't *many* of them in this particular mob, mind you, but the mob moved with a devastation and tenacity that made it seem larger—torches, revolvers, long rifles, and more.

As I soon discovered, I was too late. That Fishtown safehouse had already been discovered. O! How I shall never forget the horror in those brave faces, those souls still struggling as they were surrounded and beaten for sport, even as they were bound to be returned to bondage.

The alley . . . I can't remember which one it was. It was loud and bright with torchlight against the dark, but despite the tumult, none in those rows of tenements on either side seemed to stir.

The revolver, still safe under my cloak, felt suddenly heavy. My hands felt cold, weak. There were so many men in the posse, and there was only one of me.

I thought of my mother.

I thought of the many words I'd heard over the years, praying and pleading and petitioning for common sense and humanity from hardened hearts.

Yet it was the sight of those brave black souls, those sable heroes fighting with nothing at hand, that made something stir; it was in their eyes that I heard the Spirit speak to me.

This offense against humanity and God had to be stopped. If it meant killing these Virginia men and others like them who came and spread the infernal reach of slavery's power, then in that moment, I knew I would kill them. All of them.

And so, I raised the revolver and fired.

I don't remember clearly, after that. Someone fell. Others screamed. A pair of strong arms grabbed me from out of thin air, and before I knew it, I was careening into the dark.

"Trust me," hissed a high, breathless voice beside me. "No talking. Run!"

My heart pounded in my ears like a war drum. Where was I going? Had I failed? Who was leading me deeper into dark Fishtown streets? The sounds of the posse, still angry and clamorous, were growing slowly distant.

At last, in an alley barely wide enough for two grown men to stand side by side, my guide stopped. I was grateful for it.

In the thin sliver of moonlight that pierced the tiny

gap between buildings, I saw a woman smaller than me, sweating and panting as she leaned against the wall.

"Sir," she said, "I don't know who you are, but this is no time to be a martyr. Not while there are others to save."

At *sir*, I couldn't help but laugh in spite of myself. "Why did you save me?" I rasped, still a little breathless.

She gasped in realization. I touched a finger to my lips to quiet her.

"Because you acted," she whispered. "*Ma'am.*"

"Chloë," I said.

She straightened up. "That's Greek, isn't it?"

"This is hardly the time for a grammar lesson, and in the first place—"

"Blooming." She pointed at the sliver of moonlight high above. "You're an unexpected moonflower, Miss Chloë. Now come on. We don't have time." Then she was moving again.

"Who are you?" I asked.

"Nobody," she whispered back. "Keep walking."

When we emerged onto another narrow street and the moonlight better caught her form, I found she was a woman short of stature, just shy of five feet, with ruddy hair that fell in curls around a gentle face. But the spell was soon broken.

"Do you really want to help?"

"*Yes.*"

"Then go home," she ordered. "Leave and try to do good for the cause by other means."

"Those men deserve—" I dropped my words to a low growl then, cognizant of the late hour and the angry Virginians who may have been closer than I assumed. "Those men deserve to *die* for this crime against God and man—"

"And one gallant moonflower with a revolver's going

to do it all on her own," she quipped. "Wonderful. We have abolition already, and you haven't even left Fishtown yet."

"How *dare* you!"

But she would not relent.

"You risk *everything* that good people have built up by dashing in like that, gallant though you are. Now do you *want* to help, or do you wish to undo by your thoughtlessness everything that's been done?"

I could scarcely rebut that. The truth was, I *hadn't* considered a plan, whatever my motivations.

"But there must be *something* I can do."

"Get out. Go home. Do good where you are in your own fight against this scourge." She stepped close enough that I caught the warmth of her breath and the faint scent of roses on her dress. "And *don't* come back, damn you."

She ran off then, disappearing back into the gloom of the city at night, and was gone.

That was it: my first glimpse of Leigh Andrea Hunter. The one who would become my light.

By some miracle, I found my horse undisturbed, with no sign of the posse anywhere, and rode through the dark back to Germantown in a silence so profound, it felt as loud as it was deceptive. I stabled the horse and fell into bed, and a profound sleep, as that of the dead, soon claimed me.

Leigh had been a lookout and had had a hand in successfully moving another group of fugitives safely out of town that night. This, I learned later.

I sooner learned that there was talk of an assassin, or so the Southern partisans in Philadelphia howled. A strange black-cloaked figure who'd wounded one of their "brave heroes" who'd been sent up from Virginia to recover the people they had the audacity to call property. There was talk of a search for this assassin too. I held my breath, but in the end, nothing came of it.

I did do as Leigh told me, for a time. If for nothing else, I did it in the interest of better reflecting on *why* I wanted to help and what was within my means. The work needed doing, but I needed to better understand what the right place for me would be in that work. Quakers often speak of listening for a leading in their lives. But inasmuch as the Spirit had indeed moved me that night, I had been left twisting in the wind as to what to do next.

So I needed to be still.

I remained at Cloughmore, pondering over what I'd done and what I'd seen and listening for that leading. And it would not be terribly long before I would receive that leading and indeed go out again.

Two

Leigh

C all me Leigh.

    Six years ago, my wife, Chloë, took an accidental shortcut from 1863 to arrive in the twenty-first century. But me? This is my second time around.

I know, I know. Same name, same hometown, and all that. I mean, what are the odds?

Let me guess. The thing you're dying to know is, "What do you remember?" I get that sometimes. What do I remember from before, or at least, what did I remember back at the beginning of all this, six years back?

The answer is going to disappoint you, I'm afraid. I didn't remember much.

Yeah, yeah, I know, I know. *Fucking killjoy.*

Sorry to disappoint, but that's not how it is for me. It wasn't like I remembered anything or everything with perfect clarity from before, and I still don't. It wasn't like I somehow spoke nineteenth-century English when I was knee-high to a grasshopper or could quote you Wilberforce or Mott at the drop of a hat or anything like that at all.

What I remembered at the beginning—if *remember* is the right word for it—were the roses.

Most roses you tend to see today are rather different. They're bred for size, color, and longevity, and horticulturists have been breeding them that way since the 1870s. But there are older cultivars, from before, that are nothing of the sort. They're smaller and not as vibrant, sure, but somehow, it's always been the scent that has stood out to me the most.

"Sublime" is how they might've described it back then.

From the beginning, before anything else came up, I've always had the roses. Growing up trans and closeted, I tried to pretend I was someone I wasn't, but I couldn't completely hide it, nor could I help it. Something deep within me, very deep, would get excited and even a little wistful and sad, all at once, at the sight and smell of those old roses.

The other thing I had was the Army.

Now, I don't have anything like a long, unbroken military tradition on either side of my family, at least not any newer than the 1860s. Dad did a stint in the Army during and after Nam, but that wasn't something anybody else in the family before him had done—his parents were from Falkirk, in Scotland, and none of their people had been soldiers since the days of Bonnie Prince Charlie in the 1750s. Sure, Mom's people were samurai until 1871, but a lot of people have samurai ancestors and don't really go to war. And sure, like a lot of trans women, I enlisted in a vain effort to "man up" and escape the festering pit of gender angst that hung over me like a dark cloud. But no, there was something more.

I was looking for something. For someone.

Oh, I couldn't have begun to tell you what or whom. I just *knew*, deep down. It felt like some force beyond me was moving me.

In 2000, at the ripe old age of seventeen, fresh out of Upper Darby High School, I—the closeted daughter of a suburban, solidly middle-class doctor and librarian—joined the Army and learned to be an 11B—an enlisted infantryman. For nearly eighteen years, from starting out as a squad designated marksman to getting out as a platoon sergeant, the Army was my life, even as I simultaneously tried to run away from who I was and find the elusive thing I sought.

But the gender angst worsened over time, and my search was in vain.

After burying several close friends, being wounded enough for two of my now three Purple Hearts, and tramping Iraqi, Afghan, and Korean dirt in the name of nothing productive, I started to grow disillusioned.

It wasn't until 2016, though, during my deployment to Rojava in Syrian Kurdistan, that everything crystallized. A lot happened then, between losing my father suddenly and getting screwed out of bereavement leave; seeing the way the United States overtly and covertly screwed over the brave Kurdish women soldiers of the YPJ militia, whom we were there to aid; and watching Turkey—nominally an ally—further hamstring our mission to support the Kurdish people and fight ISIS. Finally, after surviving the disaster that was the Battle of Jisr Ibrahim, it wasn't just my combat wounds that told me I was done. I had to get out, I had to cut loose of the Army, and I had to transition or die.

The women of Rojava in general, and the YPJ in particular, have a saying: "A country can't be free until its women are free." So I started with myself and left the

Army. In the end, I never did find what I'd been looking for there.

Exhausted, scarred inside and out, in some measure of debt, and laden with insomnia, caffeine addiction, and back and knee problems, I came home to Philadelphia and tried to start over. The city, the suburbs—I know them in my bones. Things make sense here. But I'd barely been here for a year when it all fell apart again.

Mom died suddenly, in a freak auto accident just off Sixty-Ninth Street. Dad's family threatened to sue me over ownership of our house in Millbourne, and I was forced to move out in a hurry. Brynn Maclanahan, who'd been my platoon forward observer in Syria, drove out from Newtown Square with her truck, and between the two of us, a not-insignificant amount of vape juice, and the promise of *phở* and shitty whiskey at the end, we got my shit out and left the home I had thought would be my own to relatives who put bigotry over blood.

I moved in with my cousin Hiromi, down in Passyunk Square in South Philly. She was an up-and-coming photographer, had her life in much better order than I did at the time, and besides, me and her, as well as her sisters, had always been like siblings growing up. So, I moved down there and was still catching my breath—and barely managing to keep up with both physical therapy and counseling sessions—when I was recruited as an agent by the Joint Temporal Integrity Commission.

Three years later, that would be the capacity in which I met Chloë Parker Stanton, who was, by then, about six months post-displacement from 1863.

It's unclear when exactly temporal displacements began, but they've been a fact of life since roughly the early 1960s—people from the past just popping into the present, seemingly at random. The JTIC is a relatively new agency, founded by the federal government in 2000 after the duties became too great for the Department of Defense and a dozen other federal agencies to handle piecemeal. Its public-facing mission is interception, support, and resettlement of temporally displaced persons. I bought that at the beginning, but nearly two years in, I wasn't so sure anymore.

So it was amid a growing need to cut loose again that I met her.

That morning of 13 May 2020 was absolutely gorgeous. There was just a hint of light, fluffy cloud cover against blue skies. We were still squarely in that sweet spot in the spring where it's warm enough that you're not likely to freeze but cool enough that you're not sweating to death.

I'd gotten up early and gone running, the way I usually did. I ran north from Passyunk Square, cut down South Street to Penn's Landing, and made it clear out to the edge of Fishtown before doubling back and coming home through Old City and Society Hill.

I've always loved working out, particularly running, ever since I was in the Army. It's meditative. It took me a while to work back to that point, but as soon as I got the green light from my physical therapist to get back to working out—"Slowly, for your own sake," she'd said—and with the help of stretches, hydration, and compression, I returned to it eagerly and never looked back. It feels good to recover muscle tone, see the city, and put my mind in neutral, all at once.

When I got home, Hiromi was cooking breakfast. The house smelled of onions, sesame oil, egg whites, and soy.

"Hiromi, *tadaima!*" I called out. ⟨*I'm back!*⟩ When you grow up bilingual, code-switching is second nature.

"*Okaeri!*" ⟨*Welcome home!*⟩ Then, in English, "I'll be ready with everything down here when you're back from the shower."

"Roger that!"

By the time I'd showered, changed into leggings and a sundress, retied my knee brace, and thumped all the way back downstairs into the little dining nook we'd set up in the living room, she was bringing out the pot of fresh, fluffy sticky rice.

"How's it looking out there in Fishtown?"

"More and more gentrified as fuck. Seriously, more's the pity." I pulled out a chair and set about spooning out some rice as soon as she set it down. "Fucking venture capitalist vultures keep killing the spirit of this town, neighborhood by neighborhood."

Hiromi laughed, then slid a fresh mug of coffee across the table. "Damn, tell us how you *really* feel, Leigh."

"Ha." I inhaled the heady aroma and smiled. "Love you too, Hiromi."

Coffee has *always* had a way of calming me.

"Did you hear about the new art studio opening up by the convention center?"

"Mm?" I'd spooned out some omelet and was in the midst of seasoning it.

"That new collective of time-displaced artists—they finally got set up in their own space across from PAFA, on Race and Broad."

"Huh. No shit." I munched on egg and crispy kimchi, thinking back. "Oh, wait. Yeah, yeah, now I remember those guys. They were placed with a bunch of PAFA professors a year ago. Huh. Setting up on their own already. Good to know they're doing okay."

"Been wanting to go up and pick the brain of the Prussian dude who does daguerreotype. Figured it'd be a good perspective, even working in an all-digital format like I do." She pointed at me with her fork. "You ever think of hosting someone sometime?"

Here's the thing. It'd barely been three or four months prior that I'd been cleared for hosting, owing to our living situation and the circumstances of my physical and mental health recovery in the wake of that last Army tour. Hosting a displacee was something all of us at JTIC, even a glorified desk jockey like me, were eligible for and required to be prepared for, unless otherwise excused. It was simply part of the job, even if we never got selected.

How we got selected, I couldn't tell you—that happened above my pay grade. But it tended to happen with some lead time, there was plenty of preparation for all parties, and most of the time, it was a positive, if often disorienting and challenging, experience.

"It's outta my hands," I muttered into my bowl. "They haven't assigned me anyone yet, and I'm not in any hurry. 'Sides, a half-broken ex–platoon sergeant who's barely got her own shit together is hardly the ideal candidate to get some hapless—"

My phone chirped—incoming text from work.

Report to headquarters immediately, B level. Urgent. Housing assignment imminent.

"*Konchikusho.*" ⟨*Fucking hell.*⟩

I looked up and rubbed at my eyes to collect myself. On a shelf on the far wall, my family-heirloom bow sat in a halo of sunlight coming in through the windows. I felt a bit like it was quietly mocking me: *Spoke too soon, kid . . .*

Hiromi's next query brought me back to the here and now. "Eh? *Doushita?*" ‹*What's up?*›

I rose and quickly downed my coffee. "*Uwasa o sureba.*" ‹*Speak of the devil.*› Then, in English, "Good thing I'm already dressed."

Hiromi was soon on her feet. "I gassed up the Subaru on my way back from Wilmington last night. I'll wait to hear from you?"

"Probably best." I hurried into the hall to gather up my leather jacket and snag the keys from the table by the door. I muttered a hurried prayer. "*Namu Suwa Daimyojin.* Keep an eye on me, would you?" Then, squaring my shoulders, I took a deep breath and hurried out.

I headed out of Passyunk Square, up Broad Street, and on to JTIC headquarters, which lay beneath the Moyamensing Institute on Ben Franklin Parkway. Soon, I was parked deep in the bowels of the subterranean garage and hurrying out of the vehicle to the security gate. My heart was in my throat. I really would've preferred to have been left alone, but I figured the sooner I got this done, the better.

We have a phrase for it in the Army. *Embrace the suck.*

On B level, I was met by my section chief, Martha Stavridis, who seemed nearly as frazzled as I was.

"Didn't expect you so soon, Hunter."

"Figured I should get to it sooner rather than later, boss. What's the word?"

"Our displacee's from 1863—a Union Army soldier. The Army got her first, what with having vanished in the middle of an enlistment. She got fed up with waiting for proper discharge paperwork to process and broke out of Horsham Air Guard Station. Tried to steal a vehicle and gave an MP twice her size a whale of a black eye while she was at it. She—"

My eyebrows shot up. "Wait, whoa, whoa, hang on, boss. *She?* Are you sure?" I'd heard of trans men fighting in the Civil War, and the last thing I wanted was to misgender one.

"Easy, Hunter. I know. Yes, *she* is correct, according to her own words, especially once she saw her share of women in uniform. At any rate, word from on high is that you've been selected to take over and take charge of supervising the rest of her acclimation."

"Shit, okay, this is sudden, but I'm as good to go as I'll ever be. When do my prep briefings start?"

Stavridis shook her head. "No, today. You're taking her *today*, Hunter."

If I'd been drinking something, I'd have spat it out then. "Excuse me?"

Stavridis sighed and shook her head. "You're taking her immediately; we've waived the usual processes in the interest of expediting things. We'll forward you the relevant documentation and get you set up remotely for reimbursement on expenses—your information's on file, so it should be easy enough to do. But she's a problem for the Army if she can't stay put, and she needs to be out of here before too many people up our command chain *and* the PA National Guard Bureau's command chain get too uppity."

Translation: she's *your* problem now, Hunter.

I huffed in frustration and pinched the bridge of my nose, but at last, I nodded. "Understood, boss."

"Good. Let me show you in, then."

Stavridis led the way to one of the B-level secondary conference rooms, where my charge awaited.

The soldier before me was flanked by an MP on either side. Her wavy auburn hair was a little disheveled but still pulled back more or less in regulation. Her OCP-patterned digital camo, the same pattern I'd once worn, was just a touch too big. She seemed like many a train-wreck junior enlisted soldier I'd mentored over the years, except for the Army of the Potomac crest at her right shoulder where a deployment patch should go. Army policy has the original clothing of displaced soldiers burned, then replaced with uniforms to current regulation, but still, it was jarring to see the nearly 160-year-old emblem at her shoulder and the Military Horseman badge in black on her left breast pocket. At her left shoulder was the red keystone crest of the PA National Guard, but above it was a crest I had to squint to read: crossed sabers over a diagonally divided field of red and white, a number one in white above the sabers. This had to be the modern crest of the old First Cavalry Division—not our tank division of today, but the guys on horseback who'd stood off the Rebels at Gettysburg.

It was so plain. Her body language, her clenched fists, all of it—I could see she was ready, almost spoiling, for a fight. But it was her eyes that grabbed me, deep down. They were captivating. And her gaze was like *fire*.

"All right," I heard myself say abruptly. "I've got this in hand. You can all step out."

Stavridis audibly gasped. "Are you sure—"

"I'm fine," I insisted, hands raised, gesturing in reassurance. But nobody moved, and it was like the dormant ex–platoon sergeant within me rose from slumber. I felt myself square my shoulders, knife-handing—fingers and thumb held together and extended, knifelike—pointing sharply toward the door.

"OUT!" I barked. "Everybody *OUT!*"

In a matter of moments, they were all gone, and I was alone with her. Alone with a Civil War ghost in digital camo who looked at me with surprise and curiosity at what was undoubtedly an unexpected turn of events in a rough day.

"Let's start this properly. Welcome to Philadelphia," I said as calmly as I could. "This is the local headquarters of the Joint Temporal Integrity Commission. In light of the recent *developments* at your duty station, I've been selected to take you with me and personally supervise your acclimation to the present. You will lodge with me and my family while the Army processes the rest of your discharge paperwork and gets your veteran benefits rolling. It's in your best interest to play it safe and not fuck up what may still be an honorable discharge. What you do after that is up to you."

"*This* is Philadelphia?"

Her voice surprised me a little—this low, husky growl.

I nodded. "Yeah. Well, we're underground, but yes. This is Center City, and you're in a neighborhood called Stanton Square."

At the name of the neighborhood, she grew quiet. She seemed surprised, even a little stunned, to hear the name.

"I see I've got your attention," I said, softer now. "Look, I've only just been cleared for this job, and if I told you I was truly ready for it, I'd be lying. How 'bout the two of us work together, soldier to soldier, and get you through this one, huh?"

She visibly warmed at that. "*You* were a soldier too?"

"Regular Army. Started out as a sharpshooter. I was in for nearly eighteen years, but things happened and I decided to leave. Got out as a sergeant first class. Final assignment was with the Second Battalion, Fourteenth Infantry."

She seemed captivated by my tattoos. In the warm weather, I'd been trying to go sleeveless as much as I could—to keep cool, to rebuild confidence, but also to show off what was then relatively fresh ink.

"What's the matter?" I asked.

"Those roses."

I blushed but took a half step closer and extended one arm, turning it palm up so she could see the half sleeve that encircled my forearm.

"This was a good-luck charm the last time I went to war. Something about roses has always made me feel safe."

"Where'd you fight? Don't tell me the Rebs are at it again."

I shook my head. "No, nothing like that. This was Syria."

"Syria. Huh."

"Listen, we should save the war stories for later. We need to get you processed, and then I can take you home with me to Passyunk Square, down in South Philly. We might as well start where we are and figure things out from there." I offered her my hand to shake. When she took it, I quickly read the nametape and rank tab on the front of her uniform. "It's a pleasure to meet you, Corporal Shaw."

Confusion passed over her face for a moment. Then she chuckled and shook her head. "Stanton. Chloë Stanton. Company F, Seventeenth Pennsylvania Volunteer Cavalry. Women weren't allowed in the Army when I mustered, so I took my father's name as an alias." I heard the dull thump of her attempt at snapping together synthetic bootheels before she offered a slight, courtly bow. "A pleasure, Sergeant—"

I'm pretty sure I visibly flinched as I held up my free hand—thankfully, without knife-handing the poor woman.

21

I hadn't been called by rank in a while, and I sure as damn hadn't made peace with the events of my last deployment.

"No. Please, no. I'm not in the Army anymore. No rank." Then I clasped my free hand around hers, which was still closed around mine. "Leigh," I added, giving her hand a firm squeeze. "Leigh Andrea Hunter. Call me *Leigh*."

As I spoke my name, she went from quiet to downright pale. Then her grip tightened around my hand.

"As . . . as long as I may return the favor of that familiarity," she finally said. Her expression was a little strange.

Is she blushing?

"You've got yourself a deal, Chloë." It took a second longer for my brain to catch up with her earlier introduction. "Wait, did you say *Stanton?*" My heart skipped a beat. "As in the Stanton Act?"

"Yes." She sighed, with the overwhelming air of *If I had a dollar for every time I got that.* "Yes, my great-grandfather was Senator Stanton of Pennsylvania."

"Then this neighborhood's named for your . . . great-great- . . . great-grandfather, right?"

"Correct. William Penn's secretary."

I whistled. "Holy *shit.*"

She cocked her head. "Excuse me?"

"Fuck. Sorry. There's . . . there's a lot to bring you up to speed on, I know. Modern profanity included."

"Forgive me, but is it common in the twenty-first century to speak so coarsely?"

"You have no fuckin' idea." I chuckled. "Now, tell me. Did they bring your belongings down from Horsham?"

"Some," she grumbled. "Not all. The rest is lost somewhere, along with my infernal discharge papers, no doubt."

"Red tape is eternal. I'm afraid the Army hasn't changed much in that respect since your time," I offered. "But don't worry. We'll sort you out in no time."

She hesitated. Willing myself further back into *me* headspace and away from platoon-sergeant headspace, I tried my best to give her a reassuring smile.

"Trust me."

And she did.

We emerged from the conference room together to find a small crowd outside talking in hushed tones. Stavridis's expression at seeing Chloë emerge of her own volition and without being dragged was priceless.

"We're good to go, boss," I declared. "Let's get her to out-processing."

Even *more* priceless was the subtle head tilt and fang-baring grin of challenge that Chloë gave the MPs. I may have gotten a little weak in the knees there.

Yeah, I thought to myself. *You're all right by me, Chloë.*

We went through out-processing at a brisk pace— JTIC bureaucracy is smoother than the Army's, though I get that that's not saying much. We gathered the rucksack containing the handful of Chloë's belongings that had been brought down from Horsham, and after the security gate, we at last emerged into the dim, unfinished concrete cavern that was the parking garage. Without breaking stride, I slipped the phone from my pocket and dashed off a message to Hiromi.

She's a soldier. About your age. Inbound in 25.

"There." I pointed to the blue Subaru Crosstrek. "Saddle up."

". . . excuse me? Where?"

It took me a moment to register what she'd said. "Shit, *shit*. Sorry, old Army habit. I just realized how ridiculous that must sound without an actual saddle."

Chloë rolled her eyes. "My, but you're most perceptive, Leigh."

"Look, hang on." I fished for my keys, then thumbed the button to unlock and trigger remote start. "Why don't we—"

Without another word, she went on ahead of me, swung open the door, and climbed inside.

I was chuckling in spite of myself. "Shit," I muttered. "I'm in trouble." By the time I caught up and ducked into the driver's seat, she'd tucked the rucksack at her feet and buckled herself in.

"You're a quick study," I remarked.

"I've been in your time for six months, Leigh. I'm from 1863, not a lunatic asylum." She pointed at the red button on the buckle. "Besides, I can read, and it says 'Eject' right there." She reached into a cargo pocket to retrieve and don a rumpled patrol cap. For someone who'd decked an MP and stolen a vehicle in her quest to get to know this time, she certainly wasn't ignorant of regulations.

I was still chuckling as I pulled the Subaru out of the parking space, turned, and started the long climb back to the surface.

"You're all right, Chloë. I think we're going to get on well."

Her eyes were on the long rows of parked vehicles, official and personal, that sat silent and subtly spectral in sparse fluorescent lighting as we passed.

"We'll see," she murmured.

I let the silence be for a little while. Soon, we were halfway up to the surface.

"Listen, Chloë. I can't imagine what you've had to handle since coming to this time, and I can't begin to imagine losing absolutely everyone and everything I ever knew, so . . . I feel like it behooves me to say: I'm sorry for your loss. All of it."

She remained quiet for a while longer. My eyes were on the incline leading us up the spiraling stack of garage levels, but I could feel her looking at me.

"A lot of people have said that since I got here," she finally replied. "You're the first who sounds like she might mean it."

"That's incredibly generous of you."

"It's the truth," she said as we reached the gate. "I've gotten a lot of platitudes from people both in and out of uniform, and not many I can trust. I arrived on horseback, but not even my mount lived. Poor thing died of exhaustion and her wounds from Gettysburg and Brandy Station before that. Guess I really don't have anyone anymore, not from before." I heard her shift in her seat. "Say, you ever ride a horse when you were in the Army?"

"Just the once." I nudged the vehicle over the speed bumps and looked left and right, preparing to merge with street traffic. "In the battlefield in Syria, when I had no other choice. I didn't do that great in terms of horsemanship, but my training paid off and, thank gods, I didn't have to go very far."

Before she could answer, I nudged the gas pedal, turned, and we were soon coming out of the Moyamensing Institute's shadow.

"Well, officially now: welcome to Philadelphia and to

Stanton Circle." I gestured to the art deco magnificence of the roundabout crowned by Swann Memorial Fountain, statues rising out of the broad wading pool that shimmered in the midday light. We wove into traffic and did a full circumnavigation before continuing down Ben Franklin Parkway.

She gasped. "How old is this?"

"No idea, honestly."

"It's so . . . gorgeous."

"It has its moments." I pointed forward, down the road and to the southeast. "This is Ben Franklin Parkway, and down there is City Hall. That's a statue of William Penn way up top."

I caught a glimpse of her staring forward and up through the windshield in awe, eyes wide.

"City Hall's big," she remarked, "but the other ones around it, the bigger ones. The city—it isn't all this big, is it?"

At a red light, I turned to meet her gaze. "Nah. Thankfully. That's just the skyscrapers in this part of Center City, but these aren't even the biggest ones. It gets a lot lower in South Philly, where we're going."

"*Skyscrapers?*"

As the light turned green, I was eyes on the road again, guiding the Subaru on past Love Park and around City Hall and the statues, equestrian and otherwise, that lined its perimeter.

"Now that I think about it, that might be a term you missed. Right now, I think any building taller than forty floors counts as a skyscraper? Biggest ones in the world used to be here—hell, the first modern one is the PSFS Building over there, from the early 1930s. We can come up here sometime, and I can show you inside some of them."

I pointed to the left as we rounded the corner by the old Wanamaker Building. "At any rate, we lost the title of tallest to Chicago, then New York . . . I think the biggest skyscraper in the world is in Dubai now. Nearly half a mile high—more like a city in a building, at that point. Got to see it the one time I passed through on leave during my tour in Iraq."

"*Half a mile?*"

She had me smiling again. That wonder and surprise was infectious.

"Yeah. Blows even *my* mind."

Around City Hall and back down to where the southern stretch of Broad began, we passed the Union League. I pointed down Broad to where the skyline fell away.

"South Philadelphia—my home and now yours for the next little while. Like I said, the buildings are a little shorter here, and you might even recognize a few. You ever been down here?"

"A bit," Chloë muttered. Her eyes were still on the road as we pressed on toward South Street. "It's . . . it's bright."

"I guess it's all right." I waved as we passed South. "South Street's kind of a tourist trap too, but I still love it. I got my bigger tats done here, I come here for my coffee, and the indie music scene isn't too bad either."

"Coffee?" Chloë perked up. "Actual coffee, I hope."

"You're damn right." I nodded as we turned left onto Ellsworth. A couple turns later, we were driving down Federal. "Wait, you didn't think I meant chicory or peanut, did you?"

"Figured I shouldn't take anything for granted anymore."

"You're *perceptive*, Chloë. Yeah, actual coffee, not that

chicory shit the Rebels used to make in your time. I prefer making my own, but sometimes I go to a coffee shop to get some made for me, then find a nice sofa and put my feet up to people watch or read."

"My." She rolled her eyes. "Thank God some things are eternal."

"Well, I'll have to make sure to introduce you to twenty-first-century caffeination straightaway. I don't leave home without it." I pointed to the travel mug in the central cupholder.

"That's a coffee cup, isn't it?" she queried. "I don't recognize . . ."

"Travel mug. The lid has a gap for drinking but keeps the coffee in, like the cap on a canteen back in your time."

"Huh." She turned her head as I threaded through traffic and pulled in—surprisingly smoothly—to a curbside spot barely a block away from home. "Wait, are we here? Have we arrived?"

"Yeah. Yeah, we're here." I looked over my shoulder at the thoroughfare and then chuckled sheepishly again. "Oh, for fuck's sake. I just realized, this is *Federal* Street. I guess it's all the more fitting that I brought you here."

"Good thing too. Reckon I might've whupped you and tried to break myself out all over again if you'd brought me to a *Secesh* Street, Leigh."

It took me a moment to register her deadpan delivery. Once I did, I grinned.

"Chloë, you're cool in my book. Now come on. I live down thataway with my cousin, and I've sent word ahead. She'll be expecting us."

THREE

Excerpt from
Buford's Last Trooper: My War for Abolition and Union
Chloë Parker Stanton

Several months passed after my first run-in with Leigh Andrea Hunter, and on came the autumn of 1858.

The bluster and hubbub that had attended that night in Fishtown faded. Amidst the smoke and clamor of the city's industry, autumn softly descended on old Philadelphia with its magnificent crimson brush and a cool that eased the heat of waning summer.

Then there came a morning when my mother gave me some startling news.

We had just risen from breakfast and were strolling in the garden among the lilies in flower. Even though at that point she was often ill and in the twilight of her life, my mother, Hannah Archer Stanton, was a formidable woman, as were many Stanton women before her. She was brilliant and incredibly well-read, as many of us Stanton women have been. But she was also careworn, having lived in an era that offered her little room to be truly independent. Even a woman of means, as she was, had such constraints. Her brief unhappy marriage to my good-for-nothing father had broken her. Rather than continue to chip away at those constraints, she had turned inward, returning to her ancestral seat at Cloughmore and preferring to keep to her own little world and life there. Though they frequently visited, much of the rest of her birth family, the Stantons of Germantown, lived elsewhere, so for much of the time at Cloughmore in those days, it was only me, my mother, and the modest household staff.

"I've hired a new maid as your femme de chambre."

It wasn't a question—rather, simply a statement of fact. And it took me a moment to collect myself.

"Mother," I finally sighed. "*Why?*"

She leaned forward to scrutinize a lily, then breathed deeply of its scent.

"Because, child of mine, whether you like it or not, the day will come when you, too, are married. And when the happy day comes that you find a saintly husband willing to endure your freewheeling spirit, you must have the proper assistance in keeping up appearances—your own and your household's."

So *that* was her reasoning.

"Mother. *Please.* We have quite enough household staff. You hardly need to go to the trouble and expense—"

Mother raised her hand. "It is *done*, Chloë. At any rate, she comes this very day and ought to be here by now."

With that one sentence, she removed the wind from my proverbial sails. I went from flustered to completely at a loss, and as my mother straightened to regard my expression, I could tell she *knew* it.

"*Here?*" I finally mouthed.

"Here." Mother chuckled. "Come, child. Let's go make sure of it."

We went back up to the house. Sure enough, there was

word from the doorman: the new maid was waiting in the anteroom.

Imagine the surprise plainly written on my face when the door opened and I entered to find there, on the chaise, the girl from the night of the raid. It took a moment, but then the realization hit her too, for she went wide-eyed in turn and sat up in shock.

If Mother noticed, she made no intimation.

"This is Miss Hunter," she announced, gesturing to the shocked redhead, who sat bolt upright, transfixed. "She will attend you from today. She comes highly recommended by Messrs. Still and Purvis of the abolition society, among others. Apparently," Mother concluded, turning to look over the still-stunned redhead, "she's diligent, clever, and excellent conversation. Leigh Hunter, may I present my daughter, Chloë Stanton Shaw."

Leigh collected herself then and rose to curtsy.

"Ma'am."

"Her needs shall be your duty in this house and wherever she may go next, provided you perform those duties well." Mother leaned in to half whisper conspiratorially, "I'm afraid Chloë is a bit of a free-spirited bluestocking. Are you certain you can keep up?"

"Mother!" I hissed.

Leigh looked flustered, a far cry from the swift, fiery night guardian from that night in Fishtown. "I . . . I'll do my best, ma'am."

"Very good." Mother straightened up, huffed, and then turned on her heel and swept out of the room. "I'll leave the two of you to become better acquainted."

The door clicked shut. And then we were alone. I stood transfixed for a time, with eyes on the door, as if willing my mother to return.

"An . . . unexpected moonflower."

The words were hesitant, but there was just a hint of playful lilt to them. When I turned back, she was even smiling.

"Why are you—" I exclaimed, then paused, checking my passion and coming closer to hiss in her direction, "Why are you here?"

"I do believe," she fairly purred, smoothing out her skirt, "that Mrs. Shaw just outlined the nature of my employment?"

"No." I pointed at her, then down to the floor. "Why are *you, here.*"

She shrugged. "I needed a living."

She eyed me curiously then. The fire in her eyes was clear, and it seemed to draw me inexorably into its spell.

"I-I could tell Mother of where I met you," I stammered.

Her gaze did not flinch, not for a second. "And *I* could tell her the same."

She had a point.

"You make a, er . . . most persuasive a-argument, Miss Hunter," I stammered. "Perhaps we may come t-to an understanding on this?"

"Leigh," she interjected firmly. "Call me Leigh."

Curtsying was never something I did if there wasn't anyone who mattered watching. I offered her my hand instead. After a moment, she took it in hers, and we shook.

"As long as I may return the favor of that familiarity," I said.

"But what will the missus say?" Despite the words, her countenance gave no sign that she actually cared.

"Let's play that by ear, shall we?" I offered.

Briefly, she narrowed her eyes. Then she squeezed my fingers. When she smiled, something stirred in my chest.

"You've got yourself a deal, Chloë."

Now, do not misunderstand me. We did not trust each other from the beginning, even if we did have that auspicious second meeting.

For one thing, I was not used to having my movements so closely shadowed by maid, footman, or anyone else. Cloughmore had its staff, yes, but I'd been accustomed to being left quite alone much of the time; it was the space in which my spirit had thrived in those early years. So I kept my distance from her as best I could at the beginning, though to be fair, she seemed to do the same with me. She lent me a hand in the morning or set the table with the other servants, but she was always quietly eyeing me, as if studying me.

One might have said her demeanor occasionally bordered on saucy—just like that first night in Fishtown. If anything, though, this made her close presence bearable, where a perfectly demure and obedient femme de chambre would've driven me mad.

It did not remain merely bearable, of course; as one might say today, she grew on me. She didn't just stay at the estate, either; she accompanied me on excursions: first the proper, ladylike jaunts my mother would approve of, and then, slowly, farther and farther from Mother's prying eye and into town. I came to love the city better, thanks to her. And while Leigh had certainly given me ample reason to do so that first night, little by little, she showed me even more reasons to trust her.

As time passed, her presence became not just bearable but indispensable. She was energetic, and she was also sharp, witty, and eager to educate and edify herself. Mother insisted that the household staff have free rein of Cloughmore's books, and there was nary a day that I did not see Leigh with a book close at hand.

I remember the morning, during the following spring, March 1859, when we passed from hesitancy into certainty in that blossoming trust between us. It was still rather early in the day, a little after dawn, when she brought breakfast into my bedroom. I was still in my nightgown, the quilt drawn over my shoulders, and I was contemplating the view out into the gardens when she entered through the side door.

Even with my back turned, I knew her by the sound of her steps and the attending sounds of her skirt. The door opened and then shut, and there was a slight rattle of porcelain and metal on a tray.

I turned to her. "Good morning, Leigh."

Her ruddy hair fell in curls that caught the dawn light. "Chloë. Good morning. I trust you slept well?"

"Oh, yes." I chuckled, rearranging myself to make room for her to pass by me and set down the tray atop the bed beside me. "Slept the sleep of the dead."

I listened as she set things out behind me.

"I see the roses are out," she remarked. "The fragrance upon coming up from the cookhouse was sublime."

"Have the new *reines des violettes* bloomed already?" I craned my neck for a better view around the house's corner, toward the rose bed. "My word, so they have." The breeze shifted, and I caught distant notes of their sublime fragrance.

She turned as if to leave.

"Leigh," I said. "Might you stay with me awhile and chat?"

She paused. Then she smiled. "I was hoping you might say that."

I realized then that there were two cups beside the carafe, and I laughed. "You think of everything."

We sat together on my bed. I poured coffee first for her, then for myself. We shared from the simple fare.

"What did you think of Reverend Garnet's speech?" Leigh asked.

We'd made a habit of discussing our reading and exchanging recommendations of literary oeuvre we thought the other would find particularly edifying.

"It was a challenge," I began. "But I'm grateful for the recommendation, Leigh." I gestured to the dog-eared little pamphlet at my bedside. Reverend Henry Highland Garnet, a minister from Maryland who'd escaped bondage with his family, had preached to a packed church in New York on the struggles of his race under the tyranny of the slaver's lash and on the moral imperative of all to resist.

"It made me uncomfortable," I added. "And after all you and I have discussed, I am of the opinion that it is right and proper that it should evoke that feeling."

Leigh paused with her coffee cup at hand. "So. What would you do about it? Having read his call to resistance."

I looked off into the fireplace's dim embers. "Lend what little strength I have to further it on. I would be a soldier in that cause."

"Right is of no sex, truth is of no color, God is the Father of us all, and we are all brethren," she said. "Or so I've heard from people doing the work."

I smiled knowingly. "The words of the great Mr. Douglass. But . . ."

"Or so I've heard," she repeated. There was a knowing glint in her eye. She sipped at the coffee and supped on pasties with a strange, almost conspiratorial air. "But perhaps we might talk of other things? I finished *Kavanagh.*"

I refilled my cup. "What did you think of Mr. Long-fellow's work?"

"That poor Alice!" she exclaimed. "I wanted nothing more than for her and Cecilia to have been together and happy, without any intrusion by a man. They had such joy together. Why take that away?"

"They did have that joy," I replied, sipping at my slowly cooling coffee. "As did Ruth and Naomi, in the days when the judges ruled over the children of Israel."

"Amen," was Leigh's simple reply.

We were close now, almost forehead to forehead.

As I sat there, with her breath warm on my cheeks, I couldn't help but marvel at her. Spirited, clever, and every bit my equal.

I wanted this woman. Needed her.

"Leigh," I breathed. "May I kiss you?"

She flushed red, clapping a hand over her face as her eyes went wide.

I froze, transfixed, a bit horrified. "Forgive me. Have I . . . have I been too forward?"

"N-no, no." She shook her head. "It's . . . I . . . I was just thinking that I wished you might say something of the sort."

And so, we kissed.

It was a beginning.

You children of the twenty-first century have a different language about these things—and, overall, many more words, where we in earlier times had fewer or none. This is not a judgment—merely a reality. I am grateful for new words with which to express who I am and whom I love, but in those bygone times, more often, things simply *were*.

Things changed for Leigh and me as we came to understand how we each felt about other women and about each other. From awkward beginning to uncertain second meeting and now to something more.

My mother, even amid her lingering illness at the time, noted how inseparable Leigh and I had become. Of course, she did not know how we had met, but did she understand what had changed? I don't know. Yet she did recognize, in her own way, that something had changed.

"I chose well for you," she remarked one night as I rose from reading at her bedside.

If I had only had the words, in that bygone age, to explain.

"You did, Mother," I simply remarked. "You did indeed."

And so, things blossomed between Leigh and me.

We awoke one fateful morning to birdsong and long columns of sunlight streaming through the high gap in the shuttered windows. I'd fast grown accustomed to sleeping beside her—even if we did have to sometimes come up with creative excuses to explain her presence beside me so late.

What did we do so late?

Well. What does anyone do in the comforts of the bedchamber, gentle reader?

When not basking in those delights, we talked of everything and nothing, as we did on that morning. At long last, with her head still pillowed by my breast, she looked up at me.

"Chloë, you must know something."

"Yes?"

"That night in Fishtown, when I—you . . . that is, I—hm." She paused and pursed her lips as she considered her words. "You seem ready. It's time I introduced you to some friends in the cause who were unseen comrades that night. I have sent word ahead already."

I had a moment's indecision—a stab of worry. But she took my hand in hers, held it to her breast, and fixed me with the gaze of those earnest, determined eyes.

"Trust me," she said.

And so, I did. We dressed, breakfasted, and soon were off.

We found ourselves, by the end of our ensuing journey, in South Philadelphia's winding rows of houses and rambling tenements. The sun was already sinking to the west, and the city's daytime bustle had begun to subside.

When we alighted from the carriage, Leigh ushered me along with a tug of my wrist—just as she'd done at our first meeting. Thankfully, this time it was without the pressing urgency of barking dogs and angry Virginians.

"Where are we?" I asked, to no avail. Leigh did not reply, simply leading me deeper and deeper into those back streets.

The alley that opened before us was charming in its simplicity and peaceful as well. The effect was not unlike the sense of security afforded when one enters a clearing in a deep, quiet forest.

Here, Leigh halted.

"Wait here," she instructed. In the shadow of the buildings, I paused, huddled in the cover of my shawl, as she ascended the steps to knock at the door of one house. My heart pounded in my ears. Just as I began to worry, the door creaked open—just a crack—and I saw a woman peer furtively out into the street.

"Come on in." Her words seemed undergirded with a noticeable measure of urgency.

The woman saw us in and then closed and bolted the door behind her. It was not fear I felt at this but rather surprise. As my eyes adjusted, I found the interior comfortable and well-appointed, even if it was strangely quiet.

"It's good to see you again, Miss Hunter." The woman smiled. "Been a while since you were by. You're looking quite well."

"It's good to *be* back, Mrs. Still. Glad to find you looking well. It *has* been quite some time, hasn't it?" She did know this woman, then. "Mrs. Still, this is Miss Chloë Stanton Shaw. Chloë, allow me to present Mrs. Letitia Still."

As Leigh referred to me by first name alone, a bemused grin tugged at the corners of Mrs. Still's mouth. "A particularly *close* companion, I see."

"As was Ruth to Naomi," I replied, "as it came to pass in the days when the judges ruled over the children of Israel." Leigh audibly gasped.

"Amen," was Mrs. Still's simple reply. "Come along to the sewing room and sit yourselves down, ladies."

I did not yet understand the purpose of our visit to Mrs. Still's home. But soon she herself revealed it to me as we sat in a sewing room full of the tools of a prolific seamstress.

"Miss Hunter has written to us about you, Miss Shaw. She says you understand the seriousness of our cause and wish to join the Vigilance Committee."

It took me a moment to understand what was being said. I shot Leigh a stunned glance.

Trust me, she mouthed.

"I thought, madam, that the Vigilance Committee's influence and work had dwindled."

"Oh no." Mrs. Still chuckled. "Them Virginians sure wish it did."

"It would be my honor to assist you however I—"

The doorbell tinkled, and I heard the front door open. Mrs. Still sat up.

"Excuse me, ladies." She rose and hurried off.

"*The* Vigilance Committee?" I whispered to Leigh. She smiled and nodded, satisfaction perfectly written across her face. Distantly, I could hear hushed conversation in the foyer. Presently, our hostess returned.

"Follow me, ladies," she said and led the way into the parlor.

The gentleman who entered the parlor after us was tall in stature and handsomely attired, with a gaze and bearing that seemed to command respect, his countenance somehow brilliant even in the dim lamplight. We were introduced by Mrs. Still, and even after all took their seats, I could not help but look on in amazement. So *this* was Mr. William Still, of whom I'd heard such praise! This was why Leigh had brought me here!

He sat in silence for a time, carefully scrutinizing my face, as if weighing his words. Then he spoke.

"So the Bandit of Fishtown reveals herself at last."

I was surely a little pale at the invocation of that terrible night, to say nothing of how stunned I was that I had an unknown sobriquet, but I managed to maintain my composure.

"I was wrong to arrive with neither plan nor direction that night," I confessed. "Forgive me, sir. But I wish to join your cause and help forward it."

He informed me of the nature of the work and asked me many questions about what I could bring in service of the cause. Then he paused for a while to consider everything, sat up, and folded his hands.

"I understand that, aside from your ill mother, you are the de facto owner of Cloughmore House?"

"That's correct, sir."

Mr. Still sat back, steepling his fingers as he eyed me curiously. Then he looked at Leigh as if seeking a second opinion. He seemed to be weighing further words.

"Miss Hunter has written to me about the sincerity of your intentions, but I must ask you myself. Will you consent to follow instruction and not haste to needless risk without a plan?"

"I shall."

He sat up and leaned forward, narrowing his eyes.

"Our work is not easy, Miss Shaw, and it is done beyond the bounds of the nation's law. Will you devote yourself to the cause, even though the law's dictates and the opinions of many in the public are against this endeavor?"

"I shall," I declared. "Here and now, I pledge my life and all I have to this cause—to wage holy struggle to quell this offense against man and God till all men and women, whatever their color, are free."

Mr. Still regarded me impassively at first but then took firm hold of my hand to shake. I shall never forget his strength nor the passion I saw in his eyes.

"Then I bid you welcome to the Vigilance Committee, Miss Shaw. And may all our hands together hasten the day this scourge of slaveholding is broken forever."

"Amen," was my simple reply.

In this way—running messages, distracting and interfering with slave-catcher posses, guiding fugitive men and women through nighttime Philadelphia streets onward to the next way station to freedom, and contributing funds to the cause as needed—three years passed.

FOUR

Leigh

I still remember one particular morning well, one of the last few days of that May. Lingering among rumpled sheets on an aging foam mattress, I tried to collect myself before breakfast. The modest bit of ambient sunlight coming through the blinds was warm, but I felt weirdly cold. The loosely organized dresses, jackets, and old uniforms hanging in the open closet, the secured rifle locker under the window, the clutter atop the dresser, and Dad's books in the corner—newly unpacked, still stacked, and awaiting a bookshelf that had yet to arrive—all seemed far away as I lay there and tried to gather my thoughts before my feet hit the floor.

I couldn't remember everything about the dreams I'd had, but one thing was for sure: judging by how disoriented I'd been on waking, they'd most likely been nightmares.

The one thing that didn't feel far away hung above the dresser, on a bracket Brynn—my tough-talking, vape-toting Army buddy—had helped me set up the day I moved in: a little shelf that bore my household altar.

Now that had been a good day. It had felt good to swing a hammer, to build my household altar and clear a path for the gods of Suwa Shrine—who had watched over me in the field in Syria, Iraq, and Afghanistan—so they could perch and keep watch over where I slept at home in Philadelphia. It wasn't much—a little round mirror, a couple of small dishes, and a wooden amulet I'd had to order remotely and have shipped by mail—but it was something I could count on. Something that made some measure of sense.

The Suwa gods, especially Takeminakata, have always been part of my life. Mom's people belonged to a Suwa shrine back in Natori, and my Japanese-born cousins still try to attend its major festivals. But it was only during my last deployment, and in that terrible eternity of a battle among the ruins at Deir ez-Zor, that I developed a visceral, immediate relationship with those gods.

I sat up, stretched, and then bowed to the altar.

My most regular prayer, one I came up with during that last deployment when I only had a little pocket amulet, is simple.

"*Namu Suwa Daimyojin.* Keep an eye on me today, would you?"

That morning, at least, Takeminakata and Yasakatome were silent.

I might've stayed in bed longer, but there was a growing smell of coffee and fresh-baked buns wafting up from downstairs, and on the night table next to one of my utility knives and a stack of dog-eared paperbacks, my phone was pinging and vibrating at the end of its charging cable with incoming notifications. The world wasn't going to wait. It was time to get a move on. I shrugged on a hoodie, quickly brushed my hair, and wandered downstairs to the dining room to join my adoptive sibling and my unexpected houseguest.

Look, I'm not going to lie. It was pretty fucking awkward, especially during the first couple of weeks as we all settled into sharing a living space and as Chloë got her bearings in South Philly. Some things—like her disastrous first encounters with the coffee machine or the ice dispenser on the front of the fridge—I could empathize with. Other things—like race-specific language that was retrograde, if a little unsurprising coming from someone from the nineteenth century—I was a lot less patient with.

Oh, let me tell you, it was a challenge to keep the part of myself that was still Sergeant First Class Hunter from waking up—"It would be-HOOVE you!" and all. Somehow, with deep breaths and slow, measured words, I managed, only knife-handing her a couple of times. To her credit, as with the rest of life in the twenty-first century, Chloë started to learn—even if she did get spattered with coffee by my spit takes at some of her word choices along the way.

I was learning from *her* too, though I'd only just begun to realize it two weeks in. There was more to her than just a veteran or just a lost used-to-be-rich girl from nearly 160 years ago. And that was the morning, early on, that stands out in my mind as when we turned a corner.

Around then, we were all starting to get a bit more comfortable with each other—in fact, that might've been the first morning we all felt okay showing up to breakfast in our pajamas. I couldn't quite make out the conversation when I started down the steps from the attic, but when I finally made it to the ground floor, the snap of a camera shutter greeted me.

Chloë grinned up at me from her seat at the worktable,

Hiromi's fancy DSLR camera awkwardly grasped in hands still unfamiliar with twenty-first-century contours.

"Good posture." Hiromi flashed her a thumbs-up. "You're picking it up fast. But remember, watch your breathing, and be sure you don't wait for too long. It makes the hands wobble. Oh, and make sure your hands are placed properly. Here."

She rose, rounded the table, and gently rearranged Chloë's fingers till they better resembled a proper photographer's placement.

"Like that. And relax your grip."

"Relaxed grip. Hm. I'll try to remember that." She turned the camera over, digital screen up, for Hiromi's inspection. "How'd I do?"

"Huh. Could do better with composing the shot," Hiromi mused as she reclaimed the camera to squint at the image. Then she cast a glance at me over her shoulder. "But you done good. Damn good for someone who's still catching up on a hundred and sixty years of lost time. You caught something of Leigh's disheveled morning charm. Sort of a 'tatted-up disaster gay meets messy sparrow' look."

I shot my cousin a glare, but you may well imagine that I was the furthest thing from threatening right then.

"*Anda, najosutoru iginari?*" It wasn't enough to grouse in English; I had to grumble in Miyagi dialect like Grandma Shigeko used to. ⟨*Now what d'ye think yer doin'?*⟩

"Good morning, sunshine." Hiromi stuck her tongue out. "I'm just teaching Chloë how to handle a DSLR. You should be proud of her. She's a quick study!"

For a moment, I searched for some kind of snappy comeback, but that's when Chloë's eyes caught mine. There was a guilelessness that hadn't been there before.

But then, it *was* the first morning she was seeing me with my hair down and dressed in just leggings and an oversized, old Army hoodie.

"Good morning, Leigh."

Was she *blushing?* Yes, of course she *was*, but she was also in a loosely buttoned flannel with the sleeves rolled to her elbows, the old-school kind of shirt common in her original time with the long, long shirttail.

She had *powerful* thighs. They were powerful, and they were bare.

Did all Union soldiers have thighs this damn powerful? I asked myself. *And fuck, am I blushing?*

I asked myself the question, but it was pointless: Of *course* I was blushing. Butch women, especially soft butch women in casual mode, make me *weak*, dude.

"Chloë. Good, uh . . . good morning. Trust you, ah . . . slept well?"

She started a bit at that. Then, gaze momentarily falling, she nodded. "Yes. Slept the sleep of the dead."

I smirked. "Coming from someone from 1863, that's a loaded statement."

"Weren't you the one," she ventured, looking back up, her eyes flashing with challenge, "who jested about being raised from the dead by coffee yesterday?"

"Ooh. Point there." I hopped off the steps and gestured to the mug on the table beside her. "Got any more where that came from? I could use some reviving."

Hiromi gestured over her shoulder with the DSLR camera. "Kettle's hot, and I recovered your French press last night."

"*Aa, doumo sumimasen ne.*" ⟨*Oh hey, thanks.*⟩

Coffee's a ritual for me. Always has been. Back in the Army, it was one of the luxuries I tried to hang on to whenever I could: I'd have my parents send me the good stuff from home rather than the shit that came from the carafes in the DFAC at Fort Drum or the spray-dried instant stuff that I dug out of my latest MRE. Nowadays, it's my space for slowing down before the workday, or at any rate, when I'm getting my day started, even on the weekend—and sometimes, I wonder if it also helps me keep ADHD in check. It's strangely calming, rather than overenergizing like it is for others.

With French press in one hand and mug in the other, I deposited myself in the empty seat across from Chloë. Her eyes were still subtly averted.

"Gotta be a bit of a jump from the cameras you would've seen back in the day," I remarked. There was no shortage of ice that still regularly needed to be broken.

"Certainly is a darn sight more convenient to not have to hold still for an eon like we used to," she replied. Her eyeline was slowly drifting up. "Quieter, even—and I sure didn't see a flash. Plus, I reckon a camera that small's going to be portable just about anywhere."

Hiromi set the camera down beside her in favor of her phone.

"Oh, they get smaller—much smaller." She pointed to the tiny aperture of the front-facing camera. "It's kind of nuts just how small they can get. And wait till I show you my camera drone and the kind of resolution it can pack into a small lens *and* manage to fly."

Chloë sat up, leaning across the table to squint at the little dot of the lens. "Cameramen used to need assistants to carry their machines. I reckon now everyone's a camera-man! And did you say *flying* camera?"

Hiromi laughed. "I wouldn't be so complimentary. Everybody *thinks* they're a photographer now. It takes more than that to make an expert. Few people today are actually any good with a camera."

"Hah." Chloë shook her head. "Spoken like a true professional."

It was strange. It was comfortable, but it was familiar too, especially from my end. It felt a little disorienting. If only I'd known the truth of it then.

For a while, we chatted as we ate, talking of local news and the finer points of modern photography. I had a mouthful of toasted red-bean bun when Chloë abruptly changed the subject.

"Hiromi was telling me about that flag." She pointed over her shoulder. On the wall beside the fireplace, which we used as an art nook, hung a rainbow flag, beside my blue Army banner. "You're ... the term was trans ... transgender, yes?"

That nearly made me choke in surprise. You have to understand. I'm selective with how, when, and if I reveal my trans status. People like me sometimes get killed for being who we are. In circumstances as intimate as home, I'd figured it might come up sooner or later, but that was definitely sooner than I'd anticipated. And even by some-one I trust, getting outed out of the blue like that throws me for a loop. I didn't turn my head, but I *did* nudge Hiromi with a pointed elbow.

"*Omae, nani o itta?*" ⟨*What'd you say?*⟩

"Hey, hey, whoa, whoa, slow down, bucko. She asked *first*," Hiromi answered. "Besides, Leigh. *Relax*. Turns out, she's one of ours."

It took a moment for that to register.

I glanced at Chloë. "Is that true?"

Chloë turned to regard the flag, sighed, and nodded. "There's a lot of history I've missed. A lot of new words that've been made. But it isn't anything that didn't exist in my time by different names."

She turned back to the table and was all suave now. All confident.

"Besides," she said. "*Lesbian*. I like it. It evokes the glories of the classical age, and besides, I think I'll remember that one. That one's mine."

"And mine," I echoed. "Along with transgender."

Across 160 years of differing perspective, the three of us—a cisgender bi woman, a trans lesbian, and a cisgender lesbian—recognized each other as family. That was just the beginning of Chloë's education on the queer history she'd missed, but from there, it was easier.

Like Hiromi said—she was one of ours.

I think the thing that particularly blew me away about Chloë was that she was a *frighteningly* fast reader. Yeah, I know, attention spans were longer back then, and there weren't as many distractions—*blah, blah, blah, fuckin' millennials*—but holy shit, she kind of scared me.

You have to understand, we had a *lot* of books, Hiromi and I. Hiromi may have only minored in English at Ursinus, but literature had always been one of her passions after photography. When she wasn't doing photography for hire, she was an adjunct instructor at one of the community colleges out in the suburbs. Between books from college, and the books—literary, technical, and more—that she'd accumulated since, she had no shortage.

Me? Well, Mom was a librarian, so that should give you some idea. With *my* collection of art books and comics, my mother's cookbooks and poetry anthologies, my Japanese paperbacks, the shit I'd held onto from my Army career, and more, *I* had no shortage either. Then there were my mom and dad's books—mostly still boxed, some around the house and some in a locker in the self-storage facility out on Broad Street—which I had yet to work up the nerve to tackle seriously since my hurried move out of Millbourne when I lost the house.

All told, ours was a house that held a proverbial *fuck-ton* of printed word.

We'd put Chloë up in the spare bedroom on the second floor, partly because I thought it'd be bad form to make her sleep on the couch on the ground floor and partly because it had the only unoccupied bed in the house—well, sort of a futon, but bed enough. Yet because we'd never had a third housemate, we'd also used that room to store part of our combined library. Chloë was the one who asked, pretty much on the first day, if she was allowed to read the books in there, and I'm not one to tell a long-term guest they can't read anything.

So it didn't surprise me to know and see that she was reading. That being said, I *was* thrown for a bit of a loop one day in June, when I learned what shelves she'd worked her way to.

"So, I read the introduction and first few chapters of this book, *Macho Sluts* by Pat Califia."

I think steam came out of my ears. Apparently, after reading history and military manuals and books on gardening and philosophy, she'd found my shelf of erotica and kink-focused nonfiction.

"Ha, yeah." I was laughing, more than a little nervously. "What was it you said about it being more common to speak more coarsely?"

She turned to squint curiously at the shelves, gesturing with my old Califia paperback.

"Do you collect many books like this?"

"One of my oldest pleasures." I'd started to recover my composure. "Well, ah, books of all kinds, I guess. My mother was a librarian, so you might say it runs in the blood. People can be assholes, but books I can trust, even if they suck. And uh, look, don't worry. I've got plenty of books and not all of them are as risqué and bold as what you just read, just sayin'. I've got some historic stuff up in my bedroom—a bunch of Yoshiya Nobuko's work from Japan in the 1920s and even a first-edition copy of Long-fellow's *Kavanagh*, which I keep wrapped up in cloth at the bottom of one of my dresser shelves."

There was an inkling, a flash of *something* across her face. Surprise? Quiet dissociation? Whatever it was, she looked a little like she'd seen a ghost.

"What do you think of that particular tome of Mr. Longfellow's work?" she finally asked.

I had to think a moment; it'd been a while since I'd read *Kavanagh*, much less any Longfellow, but it was good to have an opening through which to briefly change the subject.

"You ask me, someone ought to write an unofficial sequel focused on just Alice and Cecilia. The whole time, I wanted nothing more than for the two of 'em to go fuck off and be happy together without a man getting in the way. They had such *joy* together. Why take that away?"

There it was again—that moment of wide-eyed shock that I'd seen come over her more than once by then.

"As did Ruth and Naomi," she said quietly. "In the days when the judges ruled over the children of Israel."

"I'm not much of one for the Bible, but I think I remember that one." I nodded. "Most lesbian book of all sixty-six, right?"

She looked up, pursed her lips, and then shook her head. "My." She laughed. "Clearly, I have a lot to learn." Then she gestured at the old paperback in her hand. "But at any rate. Califia."

"Yes. Califia." I could feel the steam coming out of my ears again. Even if it had helped me better understand my sexuality and issues of agency and empowerment, from what I imagined of Chloë's nineteenth-century perspective, Patrick Califia's writing wasn't exactly *tame* when it came to sexuality.

"That introduction was . . . eye-opening. I noted the publication date of 1988, so I understand this may be somewhat dated from the vantage point of 2020. But . . ." Her words trailed off. "It is enlightening to learn of this recent history of sexuality and of the ways that those in power have ignored or sought to repress it. And the story she tells—"

"He," I corrected. "He came out as trans several years ago. Pat is short for Patrick."

It took Chloë a moment, but she soon understood. "Huh. While they might've blanched at the material itself, Simmons and Nate would have been pleased to know one of their own would become an author."

Now it was *my* turn to take a moment.

"Comrades in arms?"

"Two of the finest men I knew in the old Seventeenth. They taught me how to, erm . . . pass, as a man, and avoid exposure and dismissal. To me, it was a necessary means to an end, to do the work. To them, well . . . it was who they were. I wonder if they succeeded in their aim to have that identity recognized."

I was blown away. Fuck, wouldn't *you* be? Sometimes it's easy to forget, but us trans folks, regardless of gender, have always been here. I'm a trans woman, Simmons and Nate were apparently trans men, but all the same, I recognized kindred spirits across a century and a half.

"Wow," I finally breathed.

"Aye," Chloë replied. "But yes, this book might not have been to their taste."

"What'd *you* think?"

Now *she* flushed. "Well, I . . ." She sputtered. "I . . . not all of what I've seen so far in these stories is my preference—"

"Nor mine," I offered.

"All the same, it is enjoyable and . . . instructive. To read stories of women with power inside and outside the bedchamber, and of the bonds they forge by their own hands . . ." She looked off, to the bright curtained rectangle that was the window. "It's . . . empowering, in ways I'm not sure I can articulate."

My heart skipped a beat. So I *wasn't* going to get my ass kicked for being some debauched libertine, after all.

"I'm glad you're finding that to be the case."

She turned, eyebrows raised, eyes hopeful. "Do you have more like this?"

I laughed. "Damn right I do."

That's how it was for a while. Chloë caught up on 160 years of missed history in bits and pieces, be it by reading, by local travel, or by experiment. Hiromi and I would trade off on playing tour guide or tutor. Hiromi was also teaching her a lot about modern photography, and to my eyes, it seemed like Chloë was finding a new passion, and maybe even a new career, little by little. At the same time, we also helped her broaden her civilian wardrobe; her Army career was coming to an end after all, and she had to plan for what came after, whatever form that happened to take.

She was better at it than even she realized. I remember one time I took her to some of my favorite places to thrift around town. When we came back, she tried stuff out while I offered pointers.

"Okay." I found myself nodding in vigorous approval as Chloë made her entrance from the central hallway. "*That* is good. That is *good*. Oh, this is outstanding. You're catching on right quick."

Below the untucked tails of a dark-blue plaid shirt, which she wore slightly unbuttoned, and a red tie, tied loosely, was her new ACU cargo pants in their mottled OCP camouflage. They were tucked neatly into boots that had wide straps and reached most of the way up her shins; these, I'd explained, were a descendant form of riding boots.

"Really now? That good?"

Again I nodded vigorously. "Oh, damn yeah. You should give yourself more credit; you're learning a whole new aesthetic and learning it pretty fast."

"Back before, in the old days, I'd've told you I looked like some kind of half-undressed officer."

"I'd argue that most off-duty Army officers nowadays wear polo shirts and questionable politics on their sleeves." I rolled my eyes and snorted. "But you? Oh, you're looking hella good. Looks like it's a good thing we did that round of thrifting yesterday."

"So, I guess I . . ." Chloë paused as she fished for the

right word. "I guess I, uhm, look—oh, what was the term? 'Hella queer'?"

She had me giggling. "Oh, wow. Damn right you do. Shit, and to think we only just introduced you to the word *lesbian* a few weeks ago. Queer ladies everywhere are in trouble, I see—oh my god, wait, I am *so* taking you to Silver Bullet today."

"Excuse me?"

"It's—it's a café I like. Tends to be pretty strongly queer in terms of the clientele and staff. You'll see what I mean—and I think it'll do ya some good to be around some of our own."

She brightened at that. "Other . . . dykes?"

I nodded. "Damn right."

"That many of us?"

"Not one hundred percent, mind you, but pretty damn significant in number. Besides, I haven't been there since you arrived, and it's about time I put in an appearance."

"Then let us consider it done."

"Sit tight," I instructed. I got cleaned up as quick as I could, changed into a fresh pair of leggings, and then we started out, down to Tenth, then north up to Bainbridge.

We came through the park, then out onto the corner at Delhi and Bainbridge. And that's when *it* happened.

How do I explain it? There's something that happens to me when I'm having a trauma flashback. Everything comes unmoored, and I'm in this weird in-between state; yanked out of the present by my ankles, my feet in Philly in the present but my head in Tal Afar in 2005 or Wardak in 2011. It takes a bit for me to come back to myself from that, especially if I don't have someone I trust—a friend like Brynn or family like Hiromi—to notice and urge me back.

Focusing on my breathing helps. Sometimes, a steadying hand on my arm helps.

But what happened on Bainbridge that day—it was like those flashbacks, but only to a point. It was more distant somehow. It didn't have the sense of danger and urgency that my flashbacks often do.

"Something wrong?"

That was Chloë's voice, closer than I expected. When I saw her, I didn't quite *see* her; what I saw was flashes of something else, as if it were superimposed upon her. It was her, but it wasn't. There was something more. Something different. Something . . . *familiar.*

"Hang on, hang on, gimme a sec. Something's not right. I feel the most bizarre sense of . . . of . . ."

I flailed, gesturing up the little alley that opened up onto South Street at its other end. Then something came over me. It took me a second to realize my feet were in motion again and I was half walking, half staggering to where the long row of houses began.

"Something's missing," I hissed, searching the rows of houses up and down the street, in vain. "Something . . ."

An echo? An afterimage? I don't know quite how to describe it. But profoundly, part of me seemed to know: *I've been here before. This isn't what it used to be.*

"Leigh?" Chloë's voice was more distant now. "What's this blue plaque?"

Blue plaques, historical markers set up by the Pennsylvania Historical and Museum Commission, are ubiquitous in Philadelphia. By the time I turned to look, Chloë was already reading the inscription.

"'William Still House. Better known for his Underground Railroad activities while living on Twelfth Street, William Still and his wife, Letitia, later lived here. They helped slaves escape to Canada and worked with noted abolitionist leaders, including Harriet Tubman and the family of John Brown.'"

I stood there in the shadow of the old rowhouse, glancing from her to the plaque, to the house, as if any of it would give me any reasonable answer for why in the ever-loving hell I was feeling the way I was.

I finally sighed. "Come on. I . . . I can't . . . just come on."

"Leigh?"

"Come *on*." I turned on my heel and started walking as fast as I could. Away from the plaque, away from the house, away from the street, back onto Bainbridge, swearing under my breath the whole way. No way was I taking that shortcut again. I tried my best to stay grounded, but that just made me feel like I was slowly going mad. It was like there was a reference missing, or something that used to be in my "memory banks" was gone.

"Leigh, for goodness' sake, *slow down!*"

"We're almost to the café, and I can't stay on this block. I—"

Her hand was on my shoulder. I turned, wheeled, flinched, and tried to collect myself all in one awkward, jumpy motion.

"I don't understand," she said. "But for all I can tell, you look like . . ."

"Like what?"

Her gaze fell again.

"Like you knew it. Like you knew it, and you saw a ghost."

"Why, did *you* know William and Letitia Still?" I winced as I heard the sharp edge in my voice.

She looked up at me, straight up, straight into my eyes, and her gaze seemed, for a moment, to pierce my soul.

"Yes," she said. "Yes, I did."

An embarrassed blush tinged my cheeks. I had to look away.

"I'm sorry. I just . . . I feel like I know that house," I explained. "I've never been up that street, I've never seen that house before, yet I feel like I know that house, and for the life of me, I don't know why."

After a while, she sighed.

"We mustn't be late. You were saying, about the café. We have places to be."

"Um, yeah. Yeah, we have places to be. C'mon, let's keep going."

We walked in silence for the rest of the way. I was too busy getting eaten up by embarrassment for having made a scene, and she was too busy taking in the details of each block we passed. If it was all going to be like this, how was I gonna survive?

I gestured at the café's sign as it came into view. "There it is."

She squinted, shielding her eyes with a hand. "Is that—is that a bullet? It looks—it looks *long*, and it isn't shaped right."

I laughed. "I'll explain later. Now come on, let's go in. I've got a hankering for some coffee."

The Silver Bullet was roomy but not too big. That was partly because who the fuck could afford that kind of rent, but also it was the nature of the space. It had been reclaimed from an old garage on Bainbridge, just enough off South to usually be devoid of tourists yet convenient enough that it was a beloved local haunt.

It was chill, it was humble. But if you dared to call it a dive, I would smack you.

Our earlier awkwardness momentarily forgotten, I found Chloë looking around in awe: the wall of found-object art, the community bookshelves in the far corner, the mishmash of refurbished tables, chairs, and sofas, and the people, many of them visibly queer. High above the coffee bar hung a pride banner that bore the image of a rifle surmounting the words *DEFEND EQUALITY*.

"Magnificent," she gasped.

I gestured her forward. "Come on."

"What can I get for you, friends?" The person working the bar didn't look familiar, but I found myself smiling at their blue undercut and the trans pride flair adorning their flannel. Chloë looked at the menu, then to me.

"I, ah . . . I defer to you," she said.

"Hm, something new for you. Oh, I know. Two Americanos and a croissant, please."

"First time?" they asked Chloë.

"Something like that."

"Well, welcome to Silver Bullet. This place is pretty rad, and it's got a way of bringing people back." Then to me, they added, "I'll get that right out for ya."

"Right on—thanks." I paid, then gestured to the end of the bar. Chloë took the hint and fell in behind me.

Now, Silver Bullet is a co-op, and that shows in a lot of different places, one of which is the decor. At the end of the bar, the staff takes turns decorating an otherwise kind of ugly-ass bit of uneven exposed brick.

And well, that's where *it* happened again.

The face on the little homemade poster belonged to a modestly dressed man in a nineteenth-century suit and necktie. His hair was close-cropped, his eyes earnest and determined. He seemed to exude an aura of "I've seen it all, you don't scare me, and I'm not gonna stop."

"William Still," I heard myself say.

"Yes." Chloë was looking up at me, but everything felt a half step distant again. "How did you—"

"I don't know," I said simply. My eyes remained on Still's. "I . . . I don't know."

I said that, yeah. But I knew.

Deep, deep down . . . I knew.

FIVE

Excerpt from
Buford's Last Trooper: My War for Abolition and Union
Chloë Parker Stanton

It was August 1859.

August in greater Philadelphia has always been notorious for its sultry humidity. It was no different in the 1850s. Now, for quite some time, Cloughmore had been my ancestors' summer seat, back before the Act of Consolidation in 1854, when it still meant something to get *out of Philadelphia* and still be in the county. Nowadays in the twenty-first century, of course, the city's bigger, much bigger, and is coterminous with the county.

So the rest of the Stanton family went elsewhere in the summertime, and we who lived at Cloughmore House were left alone to cope with the humidity the eighth month brought.

There was, sadly, one fewer among our number then. Mother's illness had seemingly abated in the late spring, but the reprieve was fleeting. By late June, the book of her life closed. Content to entertain no suitor, I made a new mission of liberation my foremost concern, remaining at Cloughmore, which I used as a haven from which to plan and await instruction in my work for the Vigilance Committee, from the Stills or others they sent. I also continued to be a guardian of my ancestors' graves, among which I laid my poor mother's bones to rest in hallowed honor.

Yet in those dark days, I still had my light and my moments of happiness. Yes, it was more of a challenge to tend the house and grounds; one by one, our handful of regular staff took leave of us and moved on. But this left Leigh and I the room to make a home together, even amid our deathly serious work. To read together, to eat together, and to delight in each other, body and soul.

That August morning, as I awoke to the gentle kiss of breeze through the shutter, I had a moment of clarity. It came as I contemplated Leigh's head of disheveled red curls, pillowed by my shoulder, and her stout, strong arms and legs entangled with mine. Her nightgown was unbuttoned, and mine was in a heap at the foot of the bed, a testament to a long, long night of lovemaking.

I would be with you forever, I remember thinking. *Through the good days, the bad days, and all the days between.*

At long last, she stirred—momentarily confused, then settling back against me, face burrowing into my breast. I held her tighter then, shifting until I'd hooked a leg around hers.

"What are you doing?" she muttered, a happy chuckle winding through the sleepiness in her voice.

"Keeping the wolves away, darling girl."

She picked her head up at that.

"You have a way of doing that, whether in petticoats or breeches." She tapped the tip of my nose. "It's one of the things I think I love most about you."

We kissed. I drank deeply of her warm, wet tongue and gentle lips.

"I would keep doing that. I would be with you forever, darling girl." My lips brushed against the folds of her ear. "Through whatever trials we may face together."

She shivered and moaned, a new, delightful tune to my ears.

"And I would be with you," she sighed. "Forever."

Our greatest trial in our fight against the slavers' power began late that October.

You may have heard tell of John Brown. His methods in the West, during the heyday of Bloody Kansas, were known to all in my time. Severe, yes, but he struck slavery at its root, and struck it hard. His raid that year, however, was ambitious and impressive, even as it was troubling in the timing, the manpower, and the outcomes it presupposed. Yet my first real inkling of it beyond the newspapers was a surreptitious knock on the back door.

Leigh came up to find me.

"There's a messenger from Mr. Still."

I rose at once and came downstairs to meet our guest. The woman who waited for us was short, just a shade shorter than Leigh. She couldn't have been more than five foot tall. She carried herself with a strength that was palpable, even from ten paces away.

The woman, who asked us to call her Moses—a *nomme de guerre*—had newly come from Maryland. She told us there was little time to waste, that we should attire ourselves for a night at work spiriting new arrivals through hostile streets and that we should come armed.

We dined together. When darkness began to fall, we went out.

I would tell you the story of that night: How we escorted a ragtag band newly come from Harrisburg by train. How we took a wrong turn and had to scatter as leaves to the wind. How Leigh and I sheltered two brave young women at Cloughmore for over a week before we could take them to the Stills, to be passed north to New York.

I would tell you of all this, but I will not. The twenty-first century does not deserve it. For has your time learned anything from a hero like John Brown, to merit hearing new tales of his children who survived?

In this way, three years passed. But it was the beginning of what a growing number of people knew was a gathering storm. In those three years, not all those we sheltered were revolutionaries. Most were simple, everyday people who took matters into their own hands and struck out for freedom. The Stills organized, and all of us, black or white, local or transient, worked at our tasks, be it scouting, cooking, recording, acting as courier, or in my case, sometimes fighting in the dark.

Then Beauregard's rebels fired on Sumter, that day in April 1861. And at last, the storm came.

Our work did not end with the onset of war in 1861 but merely moved into a new phase. There were still plenty of black folks coming north from the South on the road to freedom. But it was under different circumstances now—the Union's generals called them "contrabands" and continued to waffle on the broader question of full emancipation. Happily, though, the Southern men who used to come hunting for those who came our way had joined the Rebel Army and would have to answer to the guns of

Union men before they once again darkened Philadelphia streets.

One after another, in ones and twos and dozens and more, loyal men flocked to the Union's cause. Between industry, hospitals, and more, Philadelphia visibly became a city at war. In 1861 and on into 1862, we watched those eager volunteers enlist, train, and don the Union blue. We cheered heartily as they marched smartly in brand-new regiments, bound for the rail lines headed ultimately to the front, row upon row of bayonets glistening in the bright morning sun. Regiment after regiment went to war, and as they did, I found a growing, troubling sense come upon me.

One day, after another new unit passed on the way to war, I finally found the words for it.

"I ought to go," I remarked to Mrs. Still, indicating the blue column with a tilt of my head. "I can shoot better than any man, and at any rate, everybody else is going."

She pursed her lips, then slowly shook her head and motioned for me to follow.

"We have plenty to do right here, Miss Shaw. Ain't gonna be any shortage of folks coming north, and they still need us."

She was right, of course. Just because the war had come and the South had seceded didn't mean the current of black folk escaping north had ceased. Again, it was quite the opposite—there were more now, from Union slave states like Maryland and Delaware too. It seemed that not a day went by that we weren't sheltering one new family or interfering with the designs of slavers hunting for another.

But the war raged, and contrary to the popular wisdom that prevailed at its outset in 1861, it showed no signs of ending quickly.

"You're right," I said, hoping it sounded convincing enough. "But I can't help feeling this way."

Try as I might to ignore it, the thought would not leave me alone.

"I should go join the fight," I said to Leigh that evening at dinner. "There is work to be done, and it is out in the field of battle."

She was surprised—stunned.

"But . . . you'd be discovered, wouldn't you?"

"I risk discovery if I try to enlist here," I told her. "So I shall go to Harrisburg and try to slip into one of the Pennsylvania units forming there. Better to be among strangers if I'm to slip in undetected."

"We have *plenty* to do here."

"The slavers are *down there*," I retorted. "I *must* go, and I must go now, while the iron is hot, to strike this scourge that it may forever lie broken."

"And they'll catch you and send you back," she insisted. "Don't waste your time, Chloë. Stay here, and let us keep doing the work *together*."

"I've been undiscovered thus far, despite going out in trousers many nights for the last three years. What does it matter if I wear trousers in the Army of the Potomac or in a South Philadelphia alleyway?"

Her eyes fixed upon me, and the fear and pain I saw in them made me question my decision. In the end, though, I would not be swayed. So Leigh, my sweet darling girl who would bend to no one, at last relented.

We readied for my departure—gathering a few comforts for the journey and sending off letters to smooth the way. I could not bring myself to go see the Stills again, or anyone else for that matter. It was somewhat a question of shame, yes. But above all, it was one of clarity and duty:

with the nation rent asunder and so many men going off to preserve the Union and drive back the insurrectionist slavers, I knew my place was *there* in that crowded hour.

We decided my departure should be in the evening, to better avoid attracting attention. When that last day arrived, Leigh and I didn't say much to each other—perhaps we knew the enormity of what lay ahead, or at least thought we did. At last, when I'd saddled the horse and buckled in my scant few belongings, I turned to Leigh to offer a few parting words before my nerves failed me.

"I've made arrangements. Your place here is secure; whatever happens, this shall be your home and you shall be its caretaker. And if the Almighty wills it, upon my return, it shall be *our* home. Keep our home fires alight, darling girl. Trust me and await my return. Please."

She stood on tiptoe, fingers brushing my cheek. I was breathless even before she kissed me.

We kissed, and we kissed, and it was a glorious, bittersweet eternity. When at long last our lips parted, she took my cheeks in her hands, gazing up at me with sad brown eyes.

"Do not urge me to leave you or to go back. I will go where you go, and I will stay wherever you stay. Your people will be my people, and your God my God; I will die where you die, and be buried there. May the Lord bring a curse upon me, if anything but death separate you and me."

It took great fortitude for me not to weep myself.

"Then trust me and wait, darling girl," I urged her. Taking her hand in mine, I kissed her fingertips. "Wait for me. I shall surely return to you, though hell should bar the way."

She said no more but clung to me as if the force of her

sentiment alone would keep me there. It was only with the greatest of difficulty that we parted.

"Trust me, darling girl." The words became my refrain. "*Trust me* and wait."

And so I left her, my darling stout-hearted girl, and mounted the saddle. While I would write her every chance I had and cling to the hope of returning, fate would have it that I would ultimately never see her again in that life. Had I known, I might have stayed in bed, held her close, and been content to let the menfolk do the fighting.

But that was not the end to which my story was fated.

Ultimately, the call to strike a death blow to the scourge of slavery was stronger and seemed to carry me onward by a force far beyond myself. There were no slave catchers left to fight here; they were all in Rebeldom. It was a leading. My choice was clear.

Sitting straight in the saddle, I spurred the horse on, out of Germantown, over the Schuylkill, and onward, beyond.

Far to the west lay Harrisburg and the chance to go to war.

SIX

Leigh

It was early July—a warm, breezy day just before Independence Day.

Philly's always been hot and ass-humid in the summer,
but this day wasn't quite so bad—warm but not too hot
and not terrible weather to walk in either.

Chloë and I got an early start that morning because, at
long last, her discharge papers were ready. After we got
back from Army business with the National Guard office
at the Twenty-Third Street Armory, we had a late breakfast
and then drove out from Passyunk Square with the windows down and the city's smells and sounds hurrying past,
just beyond our fingertips.

At a stoplight in Society Hill, en route north to Market
Street, I took a moment to turn and regard Chloë in pro-
file. She was looking out at the street, her eyes darting left
and right beneath the brim of her patrol cap as if trying to
catch every little detail of the mix of old colonial brick and
modern steel and glass that lay beyond the curb. She kept

doing that, kept trying to take everything in, and it made me happy to watch.

Not that I needed any particular encouragement to look at her.

The shifting sun that filtered through the mighty oaks, birches, and ginkgoes lining the street cast dancing patterns of light and dark over her, and the browns and greens that made up her combat uniform's pattern seemed to subtly twist and shift.

Already, she was growing on me.

She was courteous to a fault, sure, and she was working like hell to make good on nearly 160 years of catching up. But she was also funny; she had this deadpan humor that just slew me every time. She was what we'd now call a nerd too, in her own way. Ever since she'd discovered lesbian fiction, I rarely found her without some kind of paperback from our home library close at hand and a notepad full of notes. A few days earlier, I'd taken her to get a secondhand tablet she could use for both reading and learning more of the ins and outs of digital life.

But that day in early July, what was foremost in my mind was something far more visceral, as my eyes followed the haphazard path of the freckles that dotted her cheeks.

God, fuck, I thought, *you're cute.*

Earlier that morning, once I'd gotten changed after breakfast, I'd gone up to my bedroom to huddle tight in the bay window's protective half circle and make an overdue call to catch up with Mac—Brynn, my old battle buddy. To her, it was all too apparent.

"So, ah . . . lemme see if I've got this whole thing straight, Hunter. You've mostly dropped off the radar for a month and a half because you've got an uptimer houseguest from the government job

that's making you miserable, and on top of that, she's with you indefinitely because reasons?"

"Yeah, Mac, that's the long and short of it. That's right about where things are."

"She cute?"

I damn well knew the answer.

But I had to bring my mind back to the here and now. "What's on your mind?" I finally asked Chloë, surely making far too much sense for how transported I'd just been, carried aloft by infatuated musings.

"I want to remember this day," she said. "All of it." With her thumb outstretched, she gestured over her shoulder at the back seat, where we'd carried the big accordion folder full of her Army records and out-processing papers that we'd gotten from the National Guard personnel clerk, along with a duffel bag brimming with the rest of her belongings, finally sent down from Horsham. "Those forms, the, ah . . . the DD 214 and the NGB 22. Those are something for bureaucracy. I want to carve a picture in my memory of this day. With my own eyes and ears and all of me."

"Yeah. True, it is pretty monumental." I drove on. "It's nearly one hundred sixty years overdue, but you made it, Chloë. You're the last soldier of your regiment to be mustered out—and with an overdue promotion, to boot."

She rolled her eyes. "Even if 'Sergeant Stanton' sounds strange on my lips." The promotion, which had been waiting in the records of her regiment for over a century and a half, had been the work of her friend Caldwell. Shortly after Chloë vanished, he'd gone on to earn his commission.

We wove around Washington Square Park. A tour group gathered around the Tomb of the Unknown

Revolutionary War Soldier. Chloë turned her head to follow it as we passed.

"It's a strange thing, you know."

"How's that?"

"I should feel naught but pride, yet what I feel most keenly is shame and disappointment for not having seen the war through."

Oh, if *that* wasn't familiar. I drew a long breath and let out a heavy sigh.

"All I can say is that, in time, you'll get used to it, little by little, even if it doesn't really go away."

She cocked her head to glance back at me as we settled onto Market.

She sighed. "It feels like cold comfort when I know I left my comrades forever, before I could help them attain their final victory."

City Hall loomed over us as we passed.

"*Their* victory was *yours*," I said firmly. Then I chuckled. "Besides, if nothing else, you can take comfort in the fact that the Army, in its infinite wisdom, saw fit to release the rest of your belongings along with your discharge paperwork."

She chuckled—a low, purring rumble—and I felt my cheeks flush. "Strangely comforting to know that red tape really *is* eternal because, apparently, it has its advantages." I caught a glimpse of her brushing a thumb over the brand-new nametape at her right breast. The DD 214 was, functionally, a certificate of life for a temporally displaced person, so she'd renamed herself.

To honor her mother's memory, she'd made the surname Stanton her own. And to remember one of the foremost abolitionist orators of her time, she'd taken a middle name.

From that day forward, she would be Chloë Parker Stanton.

Up, up, up Ben Franklin Parkway, we swept around the Swann Fountain.

She was looking my way again.

"What's up?"

"I was just thinking. Here we are at Stanton Circle again. Was our meeting really just a month and a half ago?"

"Feels like longer."

The Moyamensing Institute now stood to my left, and below it, my office. I tried and failed to completely avert my eyes. All I succeeded in doing was gripping the steering wheel way too tightly.

A month and a half. It had been a month and a half, and I'd lost myself in being Chloë's guide to the present, to the point where unless I was filing a report or requesting expenses, I didn't think too much about the commission. Time was fairly flying by. When I compared my current life to how I'd felt commuting to the office every day, it was like night and day. It was nice to feel like I didn't have a cloud hanging over my head.

I want this, I remember thinking, willing my mind back into the here and now, back into the Subaru's driver's seat, with the smell of spring and asphalt and this magnificent woman sitting beside me. *I want* this, *not* that.

Another moment, and I finally remembered to breathe.

"So, I gotta ask. Your Army career concluded honorably today. What do you think you'll do next?"

"I'm not sure, Leigh. I've never had this much from which to choose. This era isn't perfect by any means, but women have a world of greater choice than they did before. I feel . . . nigh overwhelmed by it. But I'm confident. In time, the right choice is sure to appear." She tilted her head back to peer up at me. "It always has."

We were turning now, past the Schuylkill Museum of Art's long steps and stately columns and onto Kelly Drive, by Boathouse Row. In a moment, the view opened up past the last of its quaint little buildings, and there waited a magnificent view of the Schuylkill River and its far bank, where the rail line and Interstate 76 hugged the heights beyond.

But in my mind's eye, the afterimage of the Moya-mensing Institute's long colonnade lingered. I had to deal with it—this job that was weighing on my mind and my conscience—even if I didn't want to.

"Leigh."

"Yeah?"

"Remind me. What day is it?"

I had to stop and think it over. "Second of July."

We skirted the edge of Fairmount Park.

"Bit of an anniversary, then," she said quietly. "All the more fitting to have been discharged from the Union's service on this day. Now I shall be sure to never forget it."

I thought over what she said, puzzled, trying to recall my Civil War history—such as it was—and finally realized that the answer was plainly obvious.

"Oh, fuck." I sighed. "Gettysburg. Of course."

"Aye."

I got real quiet then. I mean, who wouldn't? What do you say to someone who was at *Gettysburg*, for crying out loud? *Sorry, I briefly forgot the exact date of the most climactic battle in American history, which you happen to have fought in, and I'm too busy side-eyeing your gorgeous freckles and pretty hair, and good gods, those thighs must be heavenly—*

"That's . . . busy."

My full attention snapped back to the here and now. She was gesturing out the window to the giant messy spaghetti of on and off ramps where US Route 1, in the guise of City Avenue, crossed the Schuylkill and met the tangle of roads that entered the East Falls neighborhood.

"Oh. Huh. Yeah, um . . ." *Focus.* "So, Route One runs the length of the East Coast. I think it starts in Key West and runs all the damn way to the Canadian border up in Maine. This is just the Philadelphia bit of it."

"Huh. Can you walk it?"

I snorted. "If you like breathing exhaust and getting run the fuck over constantly. But, ah, no, there are other trails, if you really, *really* want to hike all the way to Maine. That's probably not the best one."

She shook her head. "You've lost so much in this time."

"You ain't kidding. Now hang onto your hat."

"Why—"

Laughing, I powered into the curve, under the high arches of a stone bridge, and out into a new vista.

"Welcome to Wissahickon Valley Park."

She gasped but was soon laughing, hanging onto her hat as the wind gusted through the open windows and we hurtled onto Lincoln Drive.

Lincoln Drive, starting from Kelly Drive at the south end of Wissahickon Park, isn't *short*. You kind of have to power into and through it because the traffic sure as hell doesn't stop. Through the park's green oasis, under the high arches of Henry Avenue Bridge, we drove northeast. The traffic doesn't just move fast; there's nowhere to turn around. We continued on, out of the park, practically out to the Morton district, till we could double back via

Wissahickon Avenue, and soon we reentered the park's deep, tranquil greenery.

I pulled into an almost empty parking lot, parked, and exhaled with a sigh.

"Have—have we arrived?" Chloë's voice was hushed in awe.

"Yeah! Yeah, we're here. Kitchens Lane. You can get out."

Through the open windows, the ambient scent shifted—damp earth and fallen leaves instead of gas and warm asphalt. She closed her eyes and breathed deeply.

"This." She smiled. "This is the smell I remember."

Warmth crept up my cheeks, inexorably, at the sight of her smile.

"C'mon." I beckoned for her to get out of the car. "Let's start down the trail."

We rolled up the windows, I secured the vehicle, and off we went down the wooded path. Here and there, hikers passed us. Some stared at me, but others seemed more curious about her, still in uniform and looking around at all the different details around her. Her eyes were wide with wonder.

"Why is the path asphalt?" she queried.

"Makes it easier to drive. See the cars parked up there?" I pointed to the lot that led off the trail.

"Huh. Like one of the old plank roads, I guess." She squinted, wrinkling her nose. "Why didn't we park there?"

"The members of the riding club get preference in that lot, even if the stable and park are owned by the city."

The tree line opened up, and we emerged at the Langley Stables.

"Now listen, Chloë," I cautioned. "Nice and easy,

okay? This is your first time around horses since you got here. Be sure to not push yourself too hard. Let yourself feel what you're gonna feel, and don't force yourself to go any further than you're comfortable."

We were there partly on her curiosity, partly on my suggestion. Horses aren't too common in Philadelphia in this century, but in Wissahickon Valley Park, it's pretty common to see people regularly riding the trails. I figured it was something good to do on her first day out of the Army.

Mind, one needed a membership to ride the horses stabled at Langley. But I figured that if nothing else, Chloë could at least be among familiar sights on this big day. Riding could come later.

"Grass and mud and the smell of horse manure." She breathed deeply and smiled. "I think I'll be fine, Leigh." We rounded the outbuildings and came to the fence lining the main paddock.

"Huh." I pointed at the horses—two bays and one grey, grazing in the paddock. "That's more than I've ever seen out here at one time before."

"Are there many that live here?" Even as she asked, Chloë clambered onto the fence.

"I dunno, but I think it varies a lot. Some just stable here, others are out on the trails, and still others might be in transit to and from—hey, careful there!"

She was straddling the fence now.

"Leigh, hush. I know what I'm doing, and I really couldn't care less what some rich people are going to say." With a flourish, she swung over the fence and landed inside, her boots and the blousing of her trousers getting spattered with mud. "I suppose it's a good thing this uniform is in greens and browns, eh?"

"The door's *that* way, for the record." I pointed back around the way we'd come. "It's open to the public, and you coulda just gone in. You know, like a normal person."

She spread her arms and gave a deep, almost theatrical bow. "Do I *look* normal to you, darling girl?"

Oh, but those two little words. *Darling girl.* They connected with something in my gut, just like on the day I took her to the café and had that moment of unreality on the corner of Bainbridge and Delhi. I felt unmoored. *Transported.*

I'm pretty sure I even whimpered a little.

"Fuck it." I gathered my dress hem in one hand, braced myself against the fence with the other, and climbed up, wobbling and then stumbling down into the dirt on the other side.

She laughed. "Hey, you all right over there?"

"*This,*" I huffed, smoothing out my dress and wincing a little in pain, "is why I wear leggings and boots under my dress. *Ow, dammit,* my fuckin' knee."

I'd follow you anywhere.

The thought was strange. It was the first time I'd caught myself thinking it. On one level, it didn't make any real sense. First of all, I had my job. And once we set Chloë up on her own with housing and employment, she and I would presumably part ways. There was no "follow" involved; she'd go her way, I'd stay in my lane and keep working my job, and that'd be the end of it. As the saying goes, there was no *there* there.

That *bothered* me. But how could I put into words what I barely dared to let myself think?

It wouldn't leave me alone, though: the deep, steady clarity of it.

I'd follow you anywhere.

Thankfully, the horses didn't look like they particularly cared about our unceremonious arrival. Chloë turned, squared her shoulders, and strode out into the middle of the paddock. From its feeding trough, the grey looked up as if eyeing her, and then snorted, huffed, and returned its attention to eating.

"Lunchtime, I guess," I offered. "Guessing they don't look too keen on company right now."

"How expensive is a horse now, Leigh?" Chloë's eyes were still on the horses. "I know they're less common than they used to be, but I must know how much it costs to own one."

"I dunno, but . . . they tend to be kind of expensive today. Renting them is a lot less expensive, and you can do that here, but you have to file paperwork and buy a membership online first."

A pause.

"It'd help if I had a job before I thought of such things. Money certainly makes things easier."

"Don't worry. We can work on that," I offered. "That's what I'm here for."

She turned, looked up at me, and sighed wistfully.

"Mark my words, then," she declared. "I'll be back."

"You're on." I smiled. "Now come on. Let's go around and walk out through the door. Y'know, like normal people."

I led the way through the stable and out one of the side doors. Back out past the paddock, we headed toward the tree line and the road that led to Wissahickon Creek itself. It sloped downhill gradually at first, then sharply, its surface gravelly and uneven as it wound its way down, down, down to the riverbank.

We paused there and stood in silence, taking in the

deep, powerful quiet enfolding the burbling waters of the Wissahickon.

"All right, I am convinced of it now. I feel the urge to ask."

The words took me off guard. "Huh?"

"You're—you're very watchful." She gestured up and around at the trees and the now-higher ground on the creek's opposite bank, visible through the trees. "In the city, I could understand it as general caution that any city might warrant from a watchful denizen, but even here, your eyes keep . . . flitting."

I tried to find words to explain, but they weren't quite within reach, so I gestured down the trail and started walking again. She soon followed along, looking up at me in anticipation as I tried to figure out how to put into words the answer to her question. As soon as she had asked, I knew exactly what it was she'd noticed.

Down, down, the trail turned hard, and the thin grasses and weeds gave way to the rocky, muddy riverbank. I stopped, closed my eyes, and breathed deeply.

"A few things. But I think it's the war," I finally said.

"Aye. Which one?"

I bit my lip. "All of them." I shook my head. "Well, I guess it's all one big war now anyway, isn't it?"

"I didn't hear much from the Army that I could entirely understand." She frowned, clambering up onto the first of many big, flat boulders on that stretch of the riverside. "But am I right in understanding that the Union's been at war for . . . nineteen years?"

"Ever since 2001," I answered and climbed up after her. "I enlisted in 2000 and was in till 2017."

"That's . . . a long time." She eased down till she was sitting with her legs dangling over the edge.

"Chloë, you don't understand. There are *kids* in the Army now—seventeen-year-old *kids*—who weren't even born when the war started, but they're in now. And by *gods*, they're gonna go to war in this never-ending trash fire, just like I did when I was only a little older than them, and fight without end, and . . ." I shuddered. I shook my head and tried to will myself back to the here and now. "And that's why you saw what you saw. The word is *hypervigilance*."

With a grunt of exertion, I eased down till I was sitting beside her, eyes averted, scrutinizing the fading burn marks on the backs of my hands.

"Look, I almost want to apologize that you wound up in this time. I know it might look enlightened and wonderful, but it's kind of bullshit and hellish and getting worse, too, under a veneer of progress. And not just because of the war. We're killing the planet, we're turning on each other, the rich keep getting richer, and like you know by now, people keep coming up with new ways of discriminating—"

"The tents of the homeless are proof enough," she said quietly. "This era, too, has its own needs of liberation and abolition. It's just a matter of finding the people who are doing the work."

Something came over me then. I turned my phone off and sat on it. The words were on the tip of my tongue: *This is the truth of what I know about the commission and why it exists. Yes, it's my job; yes, I'm still on the job; but . . .*

It would've been so simple to unload it all, to tell her then and there. *The Joint Temporal Integrity Commission is an attempt at correction. The United States experimented with temporal manipulation during the 1950s. You're here because it failed, fucked up history, fucked up spacetime, and people have been falling through holes into the present ever since.*

It would've been so fucking simple. Instead, I settled for the next best thing.

"My friend Brynn would love you, Chloë. She's about as radical as I've known around here—and I know for a fact that she's hiring."

Chloë looked puzzled. "Can you be so sure? That easily?"

"I know for a fact 'cause she prefers hiring fellow veterans, and she keeps trying to snag *me*. And an abolitionist who kicked ass even *before* the war? Oh, she'd snap you right up."

"What line of work is Brynn engaged in?"

"She runs a place called Red Flag Arms out of that huge former supermarket down in Broomall that used to be a local eyesore. It's a repurposed space, so it's been a bit of a fixer-upper, but it's honestly pretty rad. Part gun shop, part gun range, part sporting goods store, part event space—and that's just for starters! Eun-seok, Brynn's wife, caters food out of there too—"

"So what's keeping you from joining her?"

Ouch.

"That's the question, isn't it?" I chuckled, looking down past my feet at the softly coursing Wissahickon.

"Mm . . . my—I don't know that I have a—" I glanced at her, shook my head, and sighed. "I dunno, Chloë. I dunno."

"Seems pretty strong for an I don't know, Leigh. You talk about Red Flag with such transparent enthusiasm."

People think that just 'cause I was a soldier, I'm not afraid of anything. The honest answer is that soldiers are human, and when it comes to confronting my own bullshit, I'm kind of chickenshit more often than I care to admit.

"I've got a stable government job, even if it's kind of

bullshit sometimes. You're the one I'm trying to prioritize here." I gestured over my shoulder, back up the hill. "Besides, the sooner that happens, the sooner you can get yourself a membership here and get back to riding."

She leaned toward me, palm on the warm rock beside me, to look up at me and squint in scrutiny. She shook her head.

"Lying doesn't become you, darling girl."

Fuck, I was sweating.

"Seriously, though," I insisted. "I'm gonna put you in touch with her. Not gonna count my chickens before they hatch, but I'd say you've got this one."

Chloë sat back. "Work in a lesbian gun shop that also caters food? Next, you're going to tell me it's the focus of revolutionary activity—"

"I mean, it *is* called Red Flag." I paused. "Wait, fuck, you missed the Paris Commune, I think."

"The what?"

I wasn't much of a deep, close-in historian beyond my own family before this job. But I'd been having to educate myself about as much as I'd been educating her.

"Okay, so have you ever read the work of Marx?"

She snorted. "The German communist? Of course!"

"Okay, so the red flag was a symbol adopted by—"

"*Oh*, yes, of course! Red, like the banners from the European revolutions of 1848!"

Now *I* was a little flummoxed. "I'll take your word for it." I laughed. "Sounds like *I've* got some more I need to read up on."

"My, how the tables have turned." She laughed. Then, cocking her head, her voice a low purr, she added, "Maybe I can be as good a teacher to you on the past as you've been to me on the present, darling girl."

The deactivated phone lying under my thigh gently dug an imprint. To the southeast, my office still waited for my inevitable return. Oh, but it would've been so easy to tell her everything, right then: what was wearing on me about my job, what was troubling me enough that yes, I did indeed dream of leaving and working for Brynn.

But all I could think, looking at the woman sitting beside me—at the sandy-brown hair peeking out from under her cap, at her freckled cheeks and curious, playful gaze—was the same thing I'd been thinking that entire afternoon.

I'd follow you anywhere.

It scared me how clear and strong that current of thought was in that moment. But it was inexorable. And I know, now, what I was trying to ignore then.

It was already carrying me in its stream.

SEVEN

Excerpt from
Buford's Last Trooper: My War for Abolition and Union
Chloë Parker Stanton

My time in the service of the Union's armies was ultimately brief. If I was a soldier of any skill, it is
because of the favor and instruction of my comrades of the
Seventeenth, my friends Caldwell and Nate in particular. I
knew how to fight in the dark in winding Philadelphia
alleys and side streets; they helped me learn how to ride
and fight like a soldier.

Caldwell and Nate—Wallace Caldwell Simmons and
Nathan Josiah Yoder—came from vastly different circum-
stances than my own: the former was a teacher from
Harrisburg, the latter a farrier from a little hamlet called
Springs. They were the best of friends, almost brothers,
when I met them on my arrival in Harrisburg.

Caldwell had been elected sergeant of Company F
shortly after its formation. He came from new money, so
he had plenty of it on hand with which to ease his entry
into the company and ensure the cooperation of those who
might be inclined to disregard him. On my arrival, though

the unit had already formed, there were still would-be soldiers entering the encampment and petitioning for enlistment. I was but one of their number, and the regiment was still in need of recruits to round out its insufficiently filled ranks.

The slender, handsome sergeant waiting at the field table did not look up from his record book at first.

"I'm Sergeant Simmons of Company F, acting on behalf of Captain Lee. Your name?"

"William Hallowell Shaw." I tried to pitch my voice down, concerned with being given away by misspeaking. My voice cracked when I gave my long-lost father's name as my own. To my horror, the sergeant slowly looked up and squinted at me.

My heart pounded in my ears.

"Are you over eighteen?"

"Just turned eighteen last, ah . . . last week."

"And I'm Queen Victoria." He snorted, quickly jotting down some notes. Then he looked up again. "Show me your teeth."

I offered him a fang-baring grin. He tilted his head, sighed, and noted a few further details.

"Your occupation, Shaw?"

"Courier." It was true, in a sense.

"As of today, your occupation is trooper." He slammed the ledger shut as he rose. "I'll take you to the quartermaster sergeant for your uniform and gear, but first—follow me."

We walked through crowded camp streets till we reached a copse of trees. He looked over his shoulder. When he was satisfied we were out of earshot, he leaned toward me.

"You aren't fooling anyone," he hissed. "Your binding is slipshod, and your voice is cracking."

I could feel the color draining from my face, but then he clapped me on the shoulder and grinned.

"Lucky for you, I recognize one of my own. Fear not, for I shall teach you, Shaw. We can save the Union and help you be recognized as the man you are."

"I'm not a man; I'm just eager to strike a death blow to slavery," I replied shakily before nodding in approval. "But I entrust myself to your tutelage."

"That's good enough for me," he said. "Now then, Private. Come along."

Soon, I was wearing the Union blue, in the form of the sack coat, trousers, and cap of a private of cavalry. They were too large, of course, but then all uniforms in that time were either too large or too small. The object was not comfort but rather uniform accoutrements, as we trained and readied to go to war. After the issue of clothing and equipment, my unlikely benefactor directed me back toward his bivouac.

"Strength is to be found in numbers, Private," was all he would say. The man who awaited us in Caldwell's bivouac was short and stocky but quiet as the summer grass. He started in surprise at our sudden entrance, then huffed and settled back down, book in hand.

"Fresh blood, eh, Caldwell?" His voice was hushed, breathy and reedy. "*Uglaablich.*"

"Nate, this is Shaw." Caldwell paused, looking from me to the bookish phantom. "One of our own."

I looked to Caldwell for reassurance; he smiled and nodded.

"I am no man," I reiterated, "but I entrust myself to

your protection and tutelage in the pursuit of our common goal of union."

Nate set down his book, stood, and came closer. "Nathan Yoder of Springs. Where are you from, Shaw?"

"Philadelphia."

"That's a long way to come to enlist in a company mostly from Cumberland County. Aren't they recruiting in Philadelphia too?"

Caldwell laughed. "Nate, you aren't from Cumberland neither."

"Neither are you!" Nate cackled, slapping Caldwell on the shoulder.

"That's neither important nor relevant," Caldwell replied, smiling despite himself. "Shaw here needs our help."

"Ja, ja, woll. And he'll have it if we ever go to Washington. Isn't them Rebels down that way?" He gestured, palm open, vaguely in the direction of the capital and the seat of the war.

As I said, they were the best of friends, almost brothers, and even there as a new recruit, I could tell it was the case almost immediately. They certainly bantered like siblings.

So began my military education at Camp McClellan, in the shadow of Harrisburg. While I knew how to ride and how to shoot, I was retrained, and to that was added unit tactics and the other niceties of service in uniform. For cavalry, like all soldiers, do not tend to fight alone.

We drilled by day, studied from Poinsett's *Cavalry Tactics* by night, and waited for our orders to march south and pursue the daring Rebels. At the end of my first week, with pencil finally in hand and time at last to write, I penned a message home to Germantown.

My darling girl:

A few moments to pen you some lines, for you are most assuredly worrying for me. I am pleased to inform you that this day finds me a soldier in my nation's cause, waiting to be sent forth to battle to render justice upon the rebels and chastisement upon those unjust men whose cruelty we have so long opposed.

You must not worry unduly for me, precious heart. I am fine, eating well, and growing stronger and hardier by the day. My bunkmates are two fine men, one from Harrisburg, the other from a little town in the county of Somerset. While I am confident in my growing abilities and in the training of our regiment, I am especially trusting in their skill and watchful eye in ensuring my safety. Caldwell, the Harrisburger, is a sergeant of our company and often undertakes administrative duties in the company officers' absence. It is rumored he is in line for an officership, in time. Nate, a soft-spoken Dutch boy from Somerset, speaks little and does much and is often to be found assisting our company farrier. I hope, when this war concludes, that we may all return in safety and that I may introduce both of them to you.

Come let me kiss your lips, precious girl. May victory and abolition be swift, and may the hand of the Almighty lead me home in safety to you.

I remember I paused, just then. I had to be careful, lest the eyes of a censor fall on this page and expose me. That was the first it sunk in: I hated being called a man, but I had to play the part if I wished to see this endeavor through. Pencil in hand, I gritted my teeth and resumed.

Your ever devoted,
W. H. Shaw

PS Burn this letter when you have read it.

It was the price I had to pay.

Not long after, our regiment left Harrisburg and went south by rail—we enlisted troopers, of course, riding in boxcars with comforts little better than those enjoyed by our horses. Our destination was the capital defenses, and we arrived with much pomp, along with regiments from across the loyal states. Soon, the time would come for our skills to be further tested and honed in fire.

We first saw the elephant—that is, saw our first combat action—in Rebeldom, in the Old Dominion State at Occoquan, on December 19 of old 1862. The Union armies' cavalry arm was not yet mature then. Our leaders were more prone to use us piecemeal, to our great detriment, than to put us to any sort of effective work in the field. Much later, I learned that our regimental historian himself said, long after the war, "to be driven in was to be branded as cowards; to be captured was equivalent to dismissal; and to be killed was a *joke*."

He was right. We got a sound thrashing, over and over. But then the strangest thing happened as 1863 opened. The army's leadership changed, again and again, and so did the leadership of the cavalry arm. To once more quote our historian, H. P. Moyer, we finally had in command *"live generals."* And it was under their command, during that spring of 1863, that we of the Seventeenth began to grow into the seasoned veterans your time remembers from that crowded hour at Gettysburg in July.

Some of your people in the present century have fallen prey to the lies perpetrated by the Rebs who survived the war and sought to spin the truth to justify their wicked casus belli. They are so utterly convinced, these would-be historians, that our war was not about slavery from the beginning. I tell you now that this is preposterous hogwash.

The war had many causes, to be sure, but the insistence of the slaveholding states on safeguarding their evil practice of holding other humans in chains for the sake of profit was a major motivator for what drove that plague of treason and disunion. Rather than reform, they chose to take up arms in defense of their wicked ways and to try to rend asunder our glorious Union.

Yet it was only through the ardent, concerted efforts of abolitionists lobbying Mr. Lincoln that there was any sort of concerted response on the part of the federal government to declare the fight against slavery as a major war aim. Mr. Lincoln was late to the genuine abolition-ground, to be sure, but I shall always remember when we bivouacked at Frying Pan Farm near Chantilly and received word of the Emancipation Proclamation.

In issuing that proclamation, Mr. Lincoln may have alienated some, but he galvanized and rededicated our struggle.

There is much this present century has left undone from our time; there has been abolition, yes, but there remain injustice and inequality, especially toward the descendants of those enslaved people. But I shall always be proud that I played my small part, before and then during the war, to help them rend asunder those chains of bondage. It is now my duty, transplanted to this new time, to continue that fight in peace and help further that sacred cause that was left unfinished.

Our regiment was in a dozen skirmishes across the length and breadth of eastern Virginia after our arrival at the capital, but the terrible fight at Chancellorsville in late April 1863 was our first truly *big* fight.

I remain horrified that our leaders, or at least a significant portion of their highest echelons, could have been caught so unawares and allowed the Army of the Potomac, our army, to be flanked and driven from the field as it was that day by the secesh host. Yet I shall ever be proud, too, for it was our regiment that stabilized our army's lines and repulsed the daring advance of Jackson's vaunted secesh "foot cavalry" at the United States Ford, one of our last crossing points over the Rappahannock River.

It was after that battle that I had my own personal trial by fire, duly delivered by a Rebel ball that struck my left arm in the thick of the fighting at the ford. I'd been promoted to corporal in the prelude to that battle and was assisting in the rallying of our troopers when I was hit. Had I perchance seen the Reb who did it, I'd have surely dispatched him, but I was not able to render that recompense.

I ignored the wound as best I could, but the pain grew too severe, and I was forced to retire from the front in search of aid. Oh, but I was afraid, more than I'd been in some time. After all, while I was more likely than a Reb to get prompt medical care, were my true identity discovered by the ministrations of a surgeon, what would I do then?

I cannot begin to describe the pain. It is a terror all its own—not only to be struck in the first place but to be on the surgeon's table, prodded and cut. Amputees had access to ether in many decently sized field hospitals, but we who received our aid from stations close to the battle lines did not have this luxury. The most we could call upon was the aid of John Barleycorn—a dram of whiskey or applejack to simply dull the pain, even a little.

So whiskey was my only aid on the surgeon's table, and it did not do much. Gentle reader, I would not care to describe the infernal horror of the pain in detail, nor would I care to repeat the experience. It was, in a word, agony.

It is unclear to me just why—whether the surgeon's busyness with other patients, the haze of battle proving a distraction, or simply the hand of the Almighty—but I was not discovered when I received treatment after Chancellorsville. Soon, I was returned to camp, where I rejoined my company and sought Caldwell straight away.

He was wide-eyed when he saw me.

"Shaw, oh thank heaven, you've come back."

"By the grace of God," I replied, weaklier than I'd expected. He led me into the tent—a welcome respite, for it was some of the first we'd slept under tents in a while. I lay down on Caldwell's bedroll just in time; the strength seemed to fall out of me just then, and I lay with my head to firm earth and all else subtly spinning.

"Caldwell. *Caldwell!*"

"I'm here, Shaw."

"Where's Nate?"

Caldwell's steadying hand alighted upon my shoulder. "Nate's out assisting the farrier with reshoeing some of the company's horses. If you can believe it, the boy came out of the last fight without a scratch."

I chuckled, but it was more a dry, rasping rattle. "Without a scratch. I should've known. The lucky fool."

"Let me bring you a canteen. You sound beyond parched."

"I feel it."

I heard him rummaging. "Oh! There it is. While you were with the surgeon, the mail arrived. There's a letter from Philadelphia for you."

The world beyond my arms and legs still subtly spun. "*Leigh.*"

"Ah, finally," Caldwell declared. "There's my canteen."

"Caldwell. Read it."

Behind my closed eyes, I felt a canteen materialize in my hands.

"Drink, Corporal," he ordered. "Drink, and I'll read."

I fumbled, drenched myself a bit, but at last, was able to drink and slake that deathly thirst. The taste of blood and the surgeon's whiskey still lingered in my mouth. I felt more than saw Caldwell settle down beside me on the dirt. A grunt, a rustle of paper.

"My dear one," Caldwell read. "Received your recent letter, and I'm glad to see you have kept safe in these recent skirmishes . . ."

I would have said something witty in retort, but I simply fell back asleep, the exhaustion suddenly claiming me.

The line of mounted soldiers extended into the distance as the grey dawn broke over the Maryland country roads. It was late June 1863; I can't remember the day, as they all blurred into each other during that hard campaign. They were long days with little rest.

As I recall it, I'd barely gotten to partake of hardtack and coffee that morning, and I'd slept little more than three hours the night before. My shoulder and upper arm still dully smarted from wounds received at Brandy Station a few weeks before. Yet I rode straight in the saddle, eager to keep doing my part. We troopers of the First Cavalry Division were hard on the Rebels' trail, even as they swept north, their destination as yet unclear.

It was proving to be yet another day spent mostly in the saddle, heading for points unknown, when I spotted the rider sitting astride the shoulder of the road. I couldn't make out his words, but he was shouting—and all who passed him erupted in cheers.

At last, we drew closer, and I recognized him as the guidon carrier from Company G. He was covered in road dust, but his countenance seemed to shine.

"Comrades!" he cried, brandishing the guidon high with one hand as he steadied his mount with the other. "You are entering the mother Commonwealth's sacred soil! Hurrah for the Keystone State and Old Glory!"

A cry of exultation erupted among our ranks. This was the state line. Pennsylvania! At last, we were to fight on home soil, in defense not only of the Union but, to borrow that saying of the ancients, of our own "altars and hearths." We were not merely from all around central and eastern Pennsylvania, but indeed, Company G had been raised in that vicinity, in and around Waynesboro.

Buoyed by the new wave of purpose for the sake of the state that bore us, we rode north, and ever on. In camp that night on South Mountain, as the horses foraged, we sat warming ourselves around bivouac fires. The day had been warm, but the night seemed almost uncommonly cold.

In the dim campfire light, I read my latest letter from Leigh.

My dear heart:

I cannot begin to express how I worry for you daily. After receiving word of your wounding at Chancellorsville, I have been ever in prayer. God grant you may return safely to me, is the ardent wish of my heart. Return safely and resume the work in which we for so long toiled alongside these

*many friends and kindred souls. The uproar that followed
your apparent disappearance has, for the most part, subsided, but people still ask after you. I have, as ever, told
them nothing and simply contented myself to work, even as
I tend our home fires and await your return. I will await
you, even if it should take a lifetime.*

Your ever devoted,
   LH

Across the fire, Caldwell huddled under his greatcoat
as he cradled a cup of weak coffee, with carbine—one of
our brand-new Smiths—sitting in easy reach on its leather
sling.

"Good news from back home?" he asked.

"Good enough," I muttered, brushing a thumb along
Leigh's signature. "Good enough. I only hope it may remain so when at last I return."

"Amen," was his simple reply.

Beside me, Nate looked up, rolled his eyes, and returned to slowly cleaning his revolver.

"*Ach*, this girl of yours," he said, as much to himself as
at all to me. "You should hurry home and take her to wife
when the war ends. Take her to wife and carry on *mit der*
abolition work." Then, to Caldwell, he added, "*Gut* husband to be, *ja?*"

I didn't bat an eyelash, of course. I had to keep their
safety, as well as mine, in mind, even if being called a man
still bothered me. But my eyes fell upon that signature—
your ever devoted, LH—and I dared imagine, just for a moment, *your ever-devoted wife, LH.*

I would take you to wife, darling girl, I thought, eyes tracing
the lines wrought by her hand. *I would take you to wife and
would have you take me to wife. Even if it should take a lifetime to*

bring about, I would be inseparable from you, as was Ruth from Naomi, in the days when the judges ruled over the children of Israel.

With a wistful sigh, as if to seal that wish, I flung the letter into the fire and watched the living flames slowly consume it. I did not know it at the time, but that was it.

That was her last letter.

"*Ja, natürlich,*" I said to Nate. "When this cruel war ends and all people are free, then I shall take her to wife."

Soon the bugle sounded—lights out. And under starry, clear skies, I pondered and dreamed and tried my damnedest to conjure up Leigh's face, until sleep claimed me for too short a time.

In the distance, we could already see the enemy army's campfires, in the direction of Cashtown and Chambersburg.

We rose before dawn and broke camp. Our regiment was the first in line in the division—and in the entire damned Army of the Potomac—to enter Gettysburg the following afternoon at about four o'clock. The joyous relief on the faces of those who met us at the town diamond was palpable.

We spotted some Rebs, mostly at a distance out on the west end of town, but by the time we made it to the town diamond, we got word that they were pulling out and escaping up the Mummasburg Road and Chambersburg Pike to the west. Our division went in line to the west and north of town. We encamped in the shadow of the college, with our vidette line out at the Forney farm on the Mummasburg Road. We were not at full strength—two of our companies were on detached duty.

The locals, buoyed by our presence, came out in small groups to chat, bring reports of enemy movements nearby, and bring food and other victuals that were far superior to our meager Army fare of the past several months. I still remember well how my heart leaped at the scent of fresh soft bread and the sound of eggs that were shortly sizzling in bacon fat over our newly laid bivouac fires.

The sight of one of our benefactors, a young black woman who had brought fresh bread to my company from one of the town ovens, put me in sudden realization: there should've been many more black folks this close to Mason-Dixon, regardless of their status under the old tyrannical laws. There should have been—so where were they?

She was talking to Caldwell as I approached.

". . . not just from here but Chambersburg and other towns up the road a piece. They've been ruthless and thorough, taking away everyone in chains, marching 'em south." She pointed over her shoulder at the hills south of town. Mason-Dixon was not far beyond them, after all.

"Who?"

The word fell from my mouth as I looked on in shock, but somehow I could've guessed what was coming.

"All of us—well, damn near all of us—all the black folk the Rebs can lay hands on. Slave born, freeborn, all of us." She shook her head. "I was gonna leave, go out to York or Carlisle until it was safe again. Been hiding a couple days till y'all arrived today."

She looked tired and relieved and sleepless, as I stood close enough to converse with her. And all rightly so.

"My name is Shaw, and I promise you—I promise you we shall stop them. We shall strike them, we shall repulse them, and we shall not relent till all are free."

"My name is Annette Harris," she replied. "I'm grateful to the Lord that I hung on to see this day. I just hope you can drive all them Rebs back."

"Come, sit with us," I offered, gesturing to our fires.

She looked at the huddled groups of blue-clad troopers, smiled, and shook her head. "No. No, thank you kindly. I need to be getting back. There's someone I need to look for, and I should be there where she can find me."

I nodded. "I understand. Sounds like someone close."

Annette smiled. "Aye. As was Ruth to Naomi, in the days when the judges ruled over the children of Israel."

Now *I* smiled, recognizing one of my own.

"Amen," was my simple reply.

After she took her leave and headed back for the safety of the town, I turned to Caldwell.

"All of them," I spat. "*All of them*. The Rebs are taking *all* the black folk they find here and hauling them off?"

"That's why we're here," he reassured me. "We're going to stop them."

"One way or another, there's only one thing to do to make that happen," I said to Caldwell, gesturing down the road to where, in the slowly setting sun, we could barely make out the Rebel campfires in the direction of Cashtown.

"And what's that?"

"Kill them," I said. "Kill the accursed scoundrels."

Then, without another word, we rejoined the company in cover under the barricade on the Mummasburg Road, set to cleaning carbines, and waited.

Before us, the Rebel host, the vanguard of slavery and wrong. Behind us, little Gettysburg, but beyond, the hallowed halls of Harrisburg, the fields of Lancaster, and the spires and rivers of old Philadelphia.

And here, our division, alone against the invaders. For the moment, we held the high ground.

The sun set. The next day was Wednesday, the first of July.

When the Rebels came in the morning, we were ready for them.

We had a good, solid commanding position on the high ground, and we had the benefit of strong, brilliant, decisive leaders in the person of General Buford on the divisional level and in Colonels Gamble and Devin on the brigade level. They used our position well, laid out a carefully placed vidette line, and had eyes in all directions from not long after our arrival. The Rebels, whose cavalry was off gallivanting—as its commander, Jeb Stuart, was often prone to do—could not boast the same as the great battle started, and were, in fact, nowhere near on that fateful morning.

It was our vidette line that first caught sight of the Rebs coming in from the direction of Cashtown, as the morning dawned grey and misty, then grew clear and sweltering.

Oh, but it was *loud* and in short order too, only growing louder as the battle grew more pitched . . .

At first, I was certain that fight though we may, we'd have to withdraw, to regroup elsewhere. Then, when we'd forced the Rebs back the first time and then the second, I flattered myself in thinking that perhaps we might have held that high ground permanently. The arrival of General Reynolds and I Corps further underlined this hope.

But the Rebs were too numerous even for us, and attacking from too many directions, and even stalwart Reynolds fell in battle. We had no choice but to withdraw, fighting our way south to redeploy in new lines along Cemetery Ridge, the lines we now know the Army successfully held till the battle's end. On the first day, though, that was all yet to come, and nothing was certain.

Oh, but we made the Rebs pay dearly. For every foot, every inch, every street corner, every yard of fence, every house. They came in numbers that only seemed to grow. At times, I saw more of the enemy's men than I did our own! But though we were forced to withdraw, not once did any of us falter. Not once did I see anyone shirk.

Should I go into a grueling account of that terrible battle, that American Armageddon, when so many others have written about it at great length in all the days and years that have since passed? Should I go into great detail on the terrible sights and sounds? Should I—can I—ever do justice to what I saw? Or should I, like the Holy Ghost, speak by putting it in sighs too deep for words?

Perhaps the day will come. But for now, I shall tell you this much: after two days on the line, first in and then south of Gettysburg, as more and more regiments, divisions, and corps marched to bolster our line, the order came for us to retire south, to guard the wagon trains at Westminster, in Maryland, and to rest our tired bones for a short while.

Though we rode ever farther from the battle, its sound seemed curiously to only grow. As we sat encamped in Westminster, catching our breath, I thought of the poor black folks torn from their south Pennsylvania homes and carried off into bondage. I thought of Annette—did she find the girl she sought? I thought of the Stills—certainly they would hear of this!

And I thought of Leigh. In my mind's eye, I could still see the lines of her signature and the letter I'd tossed into the bonfire at South Mountain just before the battle, its ashes drifting as the night wore on. Would there be more letters? How would I explain this to her?

Our respite in Westminster, however, proved brief. The Rebels were nearing us again, though they'd been soundly defeated by our army outside Gettysburg. And it was thence, on July 6, having been sent with my regiment to Williamsport, that fate snatched me from old 1863 and flung me to a strange and unfamiliar time that I would have to work to make my own.

That was all of life as I'd known it. The nineteenth century, to me, as it now is to you, became the stuff of history.

EIGHT

Leigh

Even as I learned more about Chloë's battles, my own history at war haunted me, those days—the terrible memories of all those years in the Forever War. The Army owned seventeen of what should have been some of my best and most productive years, and because of geopolitics and shitty decisions by men in power who had no personal skin in the game, most of those had consisted of me getting shot at. If I hadn't made up my mind to get out because I nearly got killed, it would've been for longer. It was no Gettysburg or anything of that sort, but it was plenty terrible in its own way.

The Forever War haunted me even in dreams, and it still does. Al-Najaf in 2003, the Korengal in 2010, and Syria in 2016. The dreams were always the same, even all those years and all those miles later.

They were then, and they are now.

The surreal blur of my usual dreamscape vanishes, in dreams like this. It's so *real*. I can feel the dry desert air sucking the moisture out of me. I can smell the blood and the grit of broken concrete and swirling road dirt.

I'm there again. It's happening again. It's all *real*.

We're in the OP—a new improvised fighting position, set up in a hurry—on the west bank of the Euphrates off Jisr Ibrahim, the Abraham Bridge. I'm with my platoon commander, Lieutenant Davidian, and Comrade Nesrin, the commander of the YPJ platoon we were supporting. We—Second Platoon, Charlie Company of 2-14 Infantry— were to take one of the neighborhoods overlooking the north side of the bridgehead. The assault over the bridge went without a hitch, and for all intents and purposes, there was barely any opposition as we moved in.

But I swear, when I have these dreams, I'm there again, in the moment when it all went wrong. It registers in my gut before the incoming fire happens, a corkscrew of dread turning up my spine. I'm turning to shout at the lieutenant when the OP, a concrete structure that had to have been a garage in better times, shakes with the concussion of incoming rocket fire.

From there, everything that can go wrong does.

Our positions—Americans and Kurds alike—start to get overrun. The rocket and MG fire go from sporadic to sustained and thundering: a rising cacophony of fire and shrapnel.

Then the comms fail.

That's when it occurs to me—well, occurred at the time—that I don't want to die, because getting killed on a rebar husk in Deir ez-Zor would mean I wouldn't get to transition. As I move from point to point to check how my soldiers are faring—some alive, others wounded, and a distressing number of fatalities, especially among the more lightly armored Kurds—the thought keeps poking at me:

I'm as good as dead. But I need to transition, so I need to live. I'm as good as dead, but I want to live!

That's where it all begins—the future, my transition, my path to a life beyond the Army and getting to be seen as myself. That's where it begins, but in that moment, I don't know that yet; it hasn't happened yet, and we're all still just as good as dead. All I know is that the bullets are flying and I'm about to die having never been truly seen. With a lot of ducking and darting around corners, I make my way back to the lieutenant. My plate carrier is heavy, my shoulders are aching under the chest rig straps, and my palms are slick under my gloves.

I want to live. We're as good as dead. I want to live. We're as good as dead. I want to live.

After what feels like forever, I make it back to report. Lieutenant Davidian speaks, but I can't hear the words. Behind her, Comrade Nesrin and two of her troopers are taking potshots through mortar holes in the concrete. We're fighting, but they're fighting harder—this is their home, their land.

I want to live. We're as good as dead. I want to live.

Then I'm through the door and out into the building's broad, open central space, running to see to my next task. Instead, I'm looking straight at a Da'esh fighter who's just coming into view, leaning forward as if he tossed something—

When the grenade goes off, everything stops. The sounds, the smells, the Da'esh, the bullets, everything. By this point, I'm really desperate, so I do what I haven't honestly done in years: I pray.

Namu Suwa Daimyojin! *God of my ancestors, DO SOMETHING!*

And just like that, he's there: the god of my ancestors,

in the deep-blue hunting garb of a thousand years ago. I see myself and I am myself at the same time, so it's not that hard to look at him. His face doesn't shine, but it's resplendent. It's magnificent and a little terrifying to look at him.

You called, child of my children, and I have come.

He looks around at everything with the calm, unfazed eye of someone who's *been there*, over and over, to the point that this is in his marrow.

I want to live, but we're as good as dead. Save me. Save us all.

Trust me, he commands. *Trust me and let go.*

Another grenade's concussion tears at me, but as I return to myself, I'm not *me* anymore. Takeminakata, god of my ancestors, is a new current coursing through me—louder, brighter—and I feel myself scream, voice no longer entirely my own, moving, never stopping, drinking in the horror in the eyes of the man who thought he could kill me with a shitty Soviet leftover and in those of his men closing in behind him.

My rifle descends, butt first, toward his skull.

Korose! ‹Kill me!› I hear myself scream. *Saa, koroshite miro!* ‹Come on, kill me if you can!›

That's when I woke.

Night terrors are something else. I wake up disoriented and a little terrified. Sometimes, I wake up gasping for air, trying to untangle myself from sheets that have twisted around my arms and legs. I get less of them now, but damned if they don't still happen from time to time. Like I said, the scars of that decade and a half run deep and haven't left me.

That time, on that particular morning, I awoke crying, and I couldn't breathe. I couldn't move either, but after a moment, I realized it was a familiar arm holding me from behind.

"What are you doing?" I finally asked, tears and exhaustion in my voice.

Chloë shifted position behind me, but her arm remained steady.

"Oh, my darling girl," she finally said. "I'm keeping the wolves at bay."

We stayed there for a long time: her arm around my waist, and the cold sweat on my arms slowly subsiding. She didn't say anything, and I'm glad she didn't because I didn't quite have the words yet. Besides, she didn't need to say anything.

"You're warm," I murmured, slipping a hand down to squeeze at her fingers, which clutched at both the thin fabric of my shirt where it rode up and the gentle curve of my belly bared beneath it.

"You're . . . big," she replied. She shifted again, scooting closer, pressing against me. "And . . . you're so soft."

Soft. You have no idea what it means to be called that. For nearly two decades, it was my business to be lethal, to be sharp, all while fighting who I was inside.

"I fought like the devil for it," I finally said.

I felt her rest her cheek against my back. "You wear it well."

The nightmare's echoes, still ringing in my ears, slowly began to subside. Through the drawn blinds, the sun shone.

"Nostalgia can be a beast."

"Excuse me?"

"Nostalgia," she repeated. "You were tossing and moaning in your sleep when I found you. Surely—"

"*Oh.*" I sat up, stretched, and turned to face her. "Shit, you mean the PTSD."

"Pee-tee—what?" She looked up at me with her brow furrowed in thought, head pillowed on one arm.

"PTSD. Post-traumatic stress disorder. I told you about hypervigilance—that's part of PTSD. And yeah, that's what docs in your time called nostalgia." I rubbed the sleep from my eyes. "Nightmares about Syria again."

Her breath caught.

"Is that what it's called now?"

"Yeah."

A sigh. "I still dream about Brandy Station. And not just during the night."

It took me a moment to register the specific battle she meant. "Virginia, right?"

"Yes, ma'am." She sat up too, folding her legs, then patted at thick, uneven scars over her right shoulder, barely obscured by one of my old muscle shirts. "I shot the damn Reb down what gave me these. His ghost, however, has yet to leave me alone."

"Nor has the first Iraqi soldier I killed in Nasiriyah in 2003." A pause. "Did they ever sit you down with a thera-pist up at Horsham?"

Chloë momentarily furrowed her brow again. "A what?"

"Aw, shit. Uh, there's . . . there are people now whose job it is to help you talk through things like PTSD. There are other people like them who can prescribe medication to help too, but talking is pretty crucial either way."

"Medication? Do you take any?"

"Yeah, ever since I got out of the Army. I use CBD to help me sleep better. Obviously, it doesn't solve everything, but it helps me function." I paused, then chuckled. "The rest is coffee, snark, spite, and my winning personality."

She cocked her head in thought, then slowly nodded.

"So you still dream of your own Syrian analogue of Brandy Station."

The memory of my own voice still rasped at my ears. *Korose! Saa, koroshite miro!* I folded my arms and tucked my feet beneath me as I better rearranged myself.

"Listen, Chloë, have you ever *seen* things downrange—er, in the field—that kinda defy all sense?"

"How do you mean?"

"That day in the OP at Jisr Ibrahim, when we got overrun, I . . ."

I glanced up the wall, to the little cypress shelf that held my household altar. Chloë followed my line of sight.

"You saw the Spirit," she murmured. "Yes?"

"He was there. Plain as you are right now, and I—there's honestly—" I gestured up at the altar; sounds came out of my mouth, but I couldn't make words form.

"Leigh. *Leigh.* It's all right. Hey now." By the time I noticed, she was leaning into my lap. "I wouldn't have gone to war in the first place had the Spirit not led me to take up arms. I believe you."

Her hand was on my shoulder, her breath warm on my cheeks.

And at the sight and feel of it—her breath, her touch, her gorgeous eyes looking up into mine—I was pulled out of the battlefield memory and back into the present. *Gods*, I felt weak.

"Chloë, um . . ."

"Yes?"

"When you were in, did you ever feel like you were looking for someone?"

I don't think I really knew what I was saying, even as I said it.

"Looking? How do you mean?"

"Like . . . like there was someone you had to find, somewhere." I buried my face in my hands and shook my head. "Fuck, why am I even talking?"

"Wh . . . er, who were you looking for?" She didn't waver, but her question was gentle, even a little hesitant.

I would deny it, but I *did* know the answer, just then. It was just one among many things—little things, like the house off Bainbridge and William Still's portrait, and others I couldn't even necessarily put into words, all in the time Chloë and I had been together. I think I *did* know, but I think that's also when it started scaring me, just how clear it was.

It was her.

I frowned and shook my head. "I don't know."

She snorted, and I looked up to see her smirking. "Perhaps I misjudge, but I still think lying doesn't become you, darling girl."

I sputtered. "Wait, whoa, who said I was lying?"

She shook her head. "It's written all over your face."

She was right and I knew it, even if I didn't quite have the words for it yet. Grinning in victory, she swung her legs out and over, scrambling to the edge of the bed.

"Incidentally, I finally got to talk to your friend Brynn yesterday while you were out."

I brightened, genuinely interested but also glad for the momentary respite. My cheeks were burning.

"Your first job interview! How'd it go?"

"She'd like me to come by the range, but before that, she said she'd love to have us come have dinner with her and her wife at their home up in Newtown Square."

"Damn." I laughed. "She really must be impressed with you if she told you first."

"She said, erm, 'Hunter's less likely to chicken out this way.'"

Brynn always has been refreshingly blunt.

"Well, I'll have to talk to her and work out the timing, then, especially since the *two* of you are clearly leading the way. It'll be good to see her—and to see Eun-seok too."

"Kind of you." Chloë chuckled. "Now then, Hiromi said she would be back in town from Manhattan this morning. Shall we check in with her and then go see about breakfast?"

"Lead the way."

By the time Hiromi got back to us and we got our shit together, it was looking more like brunch. We went up to Silver Bullet and found her waiting at a table by the wide front windows, her freshly trimmed fauxhawk a strange contrast to her rumpled blazer and infinity scarf. Her shoulder bag and camera drone case were parked on the floor beside her as she nursed an Americano out of a dull grey mug.

"*Ohayo*—mornin'. About time you two stopped making out and showed up!"

"*Ome—kora!*" ⟨*You—hey now!*⟩

"You're cute when you blush." She waggled a finger at me. "C'mon, shoo. Go order something and then come back and sit. These hipsters keep making faces at me for saving you slowpokes seats."

I made faces at her too, but she stuck out her tongue. "Have your girlfriend order for you, then."

"*Baka ni shinaide, kora!*" ⟨*Stop teasing me, dammit!*⟩

"Shoo!"

We went up and ordered, and I paid for both of us. It was a little awkward to stand next to Chloë just then and nonchalantly wait for a coffee and a lox bagel without breaking a sweat. I kind of sucked at poker face in those first couple of post-Army years. So we kind of just stood there and eyed each other through our peripheral vision the whole time. I paid for us both but didn't entirely register what either of us had ordered. Was she as flustered as I was at all of this? If she was, she was doing a good job of hiding it behind a smug grin and playful gaze.

"Lox? Good choice." She sniffed at my dish. "That's an . . . everything bagel, yes?"

"Yup, ah . . . you're remembering well. What are you getting, though?"

"I saw a thing called a 'popover' and was in the mood to experiment." She gestured over her shoulder. "Though I must say that this 'kwin-noh-ah' thing might be next on my list."

I laughed. "Quinoa. It's pronounced 'keen-wah.' It's a seed, and—"

"Americano and peanut butter popovers up!"

Chloë retrieved her order from the bar, and we headed back to sit with Hiromi.

"How was the trip up to New York?" Chloë asked. "You look tired."

"Yeah. It was a pain in the ass." Hiromi rolled her eyes. "People can be so freaking ridiculous about the tiniest things, but for some reason, filthy-fucking-rich people can be even more ridiculous. I mean, I'm not complaining—to have gotten a wedding photographer gig for some big Brooklyn muckety-muck is big—but I think most of what kept me on the job was the money, even *if* the brides were queer."

Chloë's eyebrows rose. "Even among our own," she remarked, "there are difficult people."

"Ain't it the truth." Hiromi nodded, raising her mug.

"Hey, speaking of—you had an interview, right? With Mac, for Red Flag?"

Seizing the moment, I slipped out my phone. As long as it was on my mind, I figured I might as well message Brynn.

<me>: Heard the interview went well, Mac.

It took her a little while, but then:

<vapedyke>: Hello to you too, sunshine.
<vapedyke>: So that was a great interview. Your gal there is quite the pistol.
<me>: That sounds different coming from someone still in the gun business.
<vapedyke>: Cute. Anyway—you got my message, right?
<me>: Yeah, yeah.
<vapedyke>: You, me, Eun-seok, and your gal. My place, for dinner. How about tonight?
<me>: What's for dinner?
<vapedyke>: White girl stir-fry. It's my turn to cook, and my wife's promised not to laugh. I'm just really cravin' shitty drunk food like you and me and the platoon HQ gang used to make on weekends back at Drum.
<me>: Shitty seafood, expertly seasoned—ah, memories.
<vapedyke>: . . . you know you want it.
<me>: Asshole . . .
<vapedyke>: . . . you know you wannaaaaaaa . . .
<vapedyke>: Come on, platoon momma!

"I know that laugh. That's Mac, right?" I looked up and found Hiromi smirking at me.

"How'd ya guess?"

"She's the only one who can make you make those kinds of half-laughing, half-frustrated noises."

"Ha, yeah." I turned to Chloë. "You cool with going over to Brynn's place tonight?"

"I'd be glad for it, if possible."

I returned to my phone.

<me>: We'll see you when we get there, Mac.
<vapedyke>: Good to see your gal's talked some sense into you.
<me>: It isn't like that, dammit!
<vapedyke>: You show up in a moving van, and I'm kickin' your ass.
<me>: Love you too, Mac.

"All right! We're on for tonight," I said, pocketing my phone.

"Chloë was just saying." Hiromi nodded, gesturing with her mug. "If I'm not mistaken, assuming this goes through and she's got a job, that's the end of *your* assignment, right?"

Now that? That took the wind out of my sails. I glanced at Chloë, then down at the scars on the backs of my hands.

"Wow. I, ah . . . yeah. Wow. I guess that's it, isn't it?"

My thoughts were reeling. I'd barely thought of it consciously since the entire endeavor began. And now here it was—the end.

"Don't look so crestfallen, Leigh. I'm not going anywhere; I think we're all agreed on my staying with the two of you for the foreseeable future."

Yeah, but! I wanted to say. This was the clearest and most untroubled I'd been since taking my job with the commission. And now here it was—the end. I'd have to go back to my job, back to a career I really didn't much feel invested in. And as if that wasn't enough, the reality of the commission's origins just. Wouldn't. Leave. Me. Alone. Seventeen years at war for what felt like nothing, and now two years working for the organization that had literally torn a new one in the fabric of space-time in the name of scoring one over on the Russians at the height of the Cold War.

I wasn't happy with that state of affairs. Fuck, I was *scared*. But the thought of throwing it all away and taking another leap of faith also had me terrified.

"Yeah," I muttered, draining the last of my coffee. "Yeah . . ."

Hosting a displacee was necessarily intimate, close-in, guileless work, and plenty of people who hosted them remained close with them after the job was done. But there was no denying that I was feeling things that weren't entirely professional, here. Maybe this turn of events was, in fact, a blessing in disguise.

Maybe.

We chatted idly through the rest of brunch, but I was mostly tuned out. My mind was racing; there was a lot to do. I had to get the paperwork turned in to let the commission know about Chloë's change of status, probably as soon as tonight. That was good—but it meant that I'd be back to work in a matter of days. And dammit, it hurt, deep down, to even think about going back—going back to the office and the commute and the slow, gut-churning spiral of *I hate this, I hate this, I hate this* that I was only now coming to recognize, having been out of it for over two months.

After Hiromi headed home, Chloë and I sat together for a while, poking at the remnants of brunch and talking around everything.

"I could use a walk out to Penn's Landing, out to Market Street and back," I finally offered. "But do you mind if we take a detour on the way up? Not terribly far. I just want to show you something."

Chloë nodded. "Sounds good. Lead the way."

We packed up, she fell in step beside me, and soon we were on our way.

We wound our way through the back streets north of South, out until we reached the edge of the buildings, leaving the city to one side and the open sky to the other. From our right came the low mingled roar of Interstate 95. We threaded past pedestrians, people on bicycles, and locals walking their dogs, for one long block after another.

"Okay. Here." I raised my hand to halt her. "There's no light, so remember—"

"Yes, of course. Look both ways before I cross." Chloë rolled her eyes. "Don't matter if it's a horse or a car, Leigh; you can count on me to be the soul of caution."

I laughed. "Wiseass."

We hurried across the cobblestones and into the tree-lined block beyond, terraced red-brick pathways and neatly manicured bushes sitting beneath tall trees that gently swayed in the soft wind.

"This is it."

The memorial was starkly simple: four tall black walls, intricately carved, shimmering brightly in the morning sun. It's a hell of a sight on any given day. Quietly, I gestured to the footpath around the walls, and we walked around in a leisurely half circle until we were at the far side.

"The Philadelphia Korean War Memorial at Penn's Landing," Chloë read aloud from the prominent inscription. "For Philadelphia, Delaware, Chester, Bucks, and Montgomery Counties."

She paused, turning to look up at me. "Wait, so this—this is where Eun-seok comes from, isn't it?"

"Yeah. The country, and the peninsula that contains it, the one that sits right across the Tsushima Strait from Japan. I . . ." Briefly, I paused, lips pursed. "Nah, no, that's not it. No, no, that's not where I should start you off at all, is it?"

I indicated the middle space between the walls with a tilt of my head. Dutifully, Chloë followed, till we stood in the middle. At the center, four tall black columns bore long rolls of names beneath the dates 1950, 1951, 1952, and 1953.

"You've probably heard some of this already in the time we've been together, but lemme tie it all together here. Political and social issues and other things that were left unfinished in the late nineteenth century led into the twentieth century, which opened with a war bigger and more terrible than even the War of Rebellion." I slowly scanned the roll of honor on the closest column. "It was fought across many corners of the world, by pretty much every major military power of the time, and by some of the smaller ones too. Not to mention, it also had some of the earliest modern examples of targeted mass murder of entire peoples that happened at the same time: the Ovaherero, the Nama, the San, the Greeks, the Armenians, and the Assyrians. With no war quite like it having come before, at the time they called it the Great War. Today, we call it World War One." I brushed a hand over the monument's surface, sun-warmed and smooth beneath my hand.

"I think I've seen this word before—but, wait. Did you say World War *One*?"

"Yeah." I sighed. "Because things were left unresolved when it ended, and twenty million dead, along with the mass murder of civilians, apparently wasn't enough. World War Two consumed even *more* of the world, and something like seventy to eighty-five million people died. That war solved some things, but it made other things worse, and the wars just continued. The Korean War was one of the ones immediately after World War Two."

Chloë looked aghast. "World War *Two?* Twenty million? And then *eighty-five?* In wars so terrible they were called *world wars?* The Union's armies were in these wars, then?"

I nodded again, face still turned toward the column. My eyes were closed, and I was hoping to gods I could do this right. "Yeah. Yeah, we went. Both world wars, the Russian intervention, the Chinese Civil War, Korea, Vietnam, Panama, and many more since then, officially and unofficially. And now the big, long two-decade war in Iraq and Syria and Afghanistan and a dozen other places—"

"*Unofficially?*"

"*Unofficially,*" I spat. "Wars that aren't officially declared or approved, which get started on the weakest and most strained pretenses, whose veterans are never acknowledged and whose costs in blood and treasure are written off as barely an afterthought. That accounts for most American wars anymore. I was in one of those and some of the official ones. Both soldiers and civilians alike are told that the armies fight for freedom and union. After seventeen years in uniform, all but one of them spent at war, I know the truth isn't nearly that simple or altruistic."

I turned and met her eyes. She looked floored. She knew about my war, but laying it out in the context of the past century of conflicts involving the United States horrified even *me.*

"If you're going to be working for Brynn and if you

want to understand why she feels the way she does about her Army career, you need to know about these things. It's important to her politics and to mine, and it's also why I don't much talk about my veteran status with people I wasn't in the Army with. Honestly, you're gonna need to keep working to understand how it is now. Where things stand. You've got some of it already, I know, but look, this is 2020. American wars never end anymore. And while I obviously did some good things while I wore my country's uniform . . . I don't know *what* we're fighting for right now, and honestly . . . I think we do a *lot* of harm in a *lot* of places."

For a moment, Chloë appeared to be at a loss for words. Then, at last, a question formed on her lips.

"All right. So when . . . when did the Union's armies return from Korea?"

I laughed, short and sharp and rueful.

"Return? We don't do 'return' anymore. We're still there. Brynn did a tour of duty there, and that's how she met her wife. Hell, *I* did a tour of duty there with the Second Infantry Division, nearly a decade ago now."

She looked from me to her feet, to the gleaming black sweep of the monument around her. If any further questions happened to come to her, she didn't raise them.

After a while, hand gently brushing at her shoulder, I gestured her forward through the park, back in the direction of Penn's Landing.

"C'mon," I said. "Let's keep going."

The broad river walk overlooking the Delaware was lively, but not too crowded. Here and there, local musicians sat—here a freestyler, there an itinerant trombonist with case open and a smattering of dimes glistening in the midday sun. The smell of *döner* and Chinese food wafted from nearby stands. Joggers hurried past. Far off over the water, the old battleship *New Jersey* rode at anchor on the Camden side of the river, along the shore of its namesake state.

"Penny for your thoughts, darling girl?"

Chloë was looking up at me. My heart melted all over again. *Darling girl.* It still connected squarely with something deep down inside me.

"I keep saying this." I sighed, my eyeline falling. "But I feel like apologizing that you came to a time this uncivilized and utterly bullshit."

"I dunno," she said after a pause. "I think there are some redeeming things about it, all the same."

She was looking at me.

"Eh, maybe," I muttered. Then, trying to aim for a note of hope, I switched topics. "I have every reason to believe you're gonna get this job, even if you still have to go to the range to make it official. That means . . ."

Deep breath, Platoon Momma, I thought, steeling myself. *Deep breath. Come on.*

"That means," I concluded, "that I can turn in the paperwork and make it official that you're cleared to enter twenty-first-century society in earnest."

"Is it—my, is that—does that mean, then, that we have run our course?"

"Yeah. Well—sorta. We've run our course with the commission's demands, just as soon as I turn in the papers. What you do from there is up to you."

We were walking again, coming up on Chestnut Street and the amphitheater looming below, where the river walk descended into large stone steps. The Ben Franklin Bridge stood sentinel in the middle distance.

"You ready for the big, bad twenty-first century?" I asked her.

She laughed. "Hella ready. Although . . ."

"Mm?"

"I trust I will not have run my course with you?"

Oof. All over again, I stopped in my tracks.

"Honestly," I said, steadier than I had thought I could manage, "I feel the same about you, Chloë. I don't want to go back to work, but I really want to keep you in my life too. You're—you're somethin' else."

She smirked and gestured for us to sit on a nearby bench.

"I'll take that as a compliment, I think," she purred approvingly. "You yourself are also . . . somethin' else."

"Ha. High praise."

We sat in silence for a while, people watching as the world went by around us, and sometimes stealing glances at each other. Seagulls wheeled high overhead. In the bushes lining the path to the amphitheater, sparrows chirped in little brown blurs of feathered motion.

"In all seriousness, Leigh. I'm glad to have the chance to stay with you. You are . . . erm . . . you understand."

I buried my face in my hands. "Nah, I'm just some lost broad who doesn't even know where the fuck she wants to take her life next. And besides, what do I know? You fought at Gettysburg and Brandy Station—"

"And *you* were at places I couldn't even have imagined, in wars bloodier than I could've conceived: Tal Afar and Al-Najaf, Raqqa and Deir ez-Zor and in the Korengal," she interjected gently but firmly. "We have both seen the elephant. Not just that, but you've helped me finally name— and in doing so, better understand—who I am. 'Lesbian'— the name evokes the ancients, but to know that it is an identity, an experience, something that other people don't just think about, that they write of it, read of it, and live it under the sun—why, that has meant far more than I might express."

Her hand was at my shoulder, and she'd turned, knee brushing against mine.

I looked up. My eyes swam with tears.

Her auburn hair, the freckles on her ruddy cheeks, the warmth of her strong hand on my shoulder.

She was magnificent.

Kiss me, dammit.

"Leigh," she murmured. The swagger, the bravado—it was all gone, and she was just one woman, guileless and open.

"Yeah?"

"May I kiss you?"

NINE

Chloë

A nd so, gentle reader, at long last my story comes to the present time and the present century.

From the aftermath of the great American Armageddon that was our clash of arms at Gettysburg, amid vidette duty on the eve of the battle at Williamsport in Maryland, I arrived in the twenty-first century in the proverbial twinkling of an eye, set adrift as if tossed by the Almighty onto the sands of some faraway coast.

Yet rather than a landing upon Prospero's mystic shore, my place of arrival was unceremonious and mundane, on the shoulder of a highway in Malvern, Pennsylvania, on hot asphalt among speeding cars and buses. It was there that I was intercepted by the powers that be—first by the constabulary, then by the Joint Temporal Integrity Commission, and then the Army—in the late days of December 2019.

The rest of my tale, dear reader, is by now familiar to you.

When I think of it, the days before my displacement in

time grow increasingly hazy, like the scenes of some far-away fairyland, when compared to my new world and time. Was I there at Cloughmore House, in the halls of my sinful, slaveholding ancestors, working to break the abomination of slavery once and for all? Was I in the street with Moses the Marylander, fighting the bounty hunters who came north to frustrate our cause? Was I present and in the ranks of the Union's defenders in the old days before and during the Rebellion, or did I simply dream it all and awake, fully formed, in this new time, like some latter-day sleeping Galatea?

But of course, I did not dream it at all. I was there. I did all those things. I am a child of that long-gone time, and it was the age that bore me.

I am tempted, sorely, to long for it. It was a seemingly simpler, more genteel time, without the bustle and complexity and disorder of this new century. But invariably I pause, and my enthusiasm is soon checked when I remember its darkness. The scourge of chattel slavery that the Stills and so many others worked tirelessly to destroy. The systematic subjugation of the fairer sex, in law and in garb. The terrible thunder of cannons and the trembling of earth under vast armies' inexorable tread, tramping feet and pounding, massed hoofbeats.

Don't let your contemporary loudmouths and wise-acres convince you otherwise, dear reader. That time was no utopia.

But some of what I left behind I did long for. My great-grandfather's books or my great-grandmother's rose beds. The familiar faces around Germantown. The Stills. My poor mother. My dear comrades in the old Seventeenth, particularly Caldwell and Nate.

But that was not all.

And as I continued to adapt to the present—to the freedom to wear trousers unhindered, to the convenience of tablets and smartphones, to going and coming as I pleased openly, without worrying about a lack of escort, to learning to love a reborn Philadelphia with green boulevards and blue skies, and to recognizing the injustices that cried out for redress—I found myself wondering:

Had I really left my darling girl behind?

In many ways, Leigh-the-soldier was not the same woman, to be sure. The woman I'd loved and left behind was a short, strong woman with curly red hair. She was of humble roots but uncommonly driven in the pursuit of learning. She was outspoken, sharp, and brave.

By contrast, Leigh-the-soldier was a statuesque, raven-haired Amazon with facial piercings and colorful tattoos, born in this era and steeped in the best and worst of what made it unique. She was an oft profane, occasionally confusing Japanese American who, in her own time, had served the Union. She was just as scarred by war as I was, if not more. And I found her irresistibly familiar: in the little things, in things not directly seen but rather noticed in the periphery, more perceived than directly observed. Her plain speech, her love of books, and her love of roses were but the first among many. She too was kind, funny, and uncommonly brave. The thousand and one little coincidences that surrounded our time together there in South Philadelphia only seemed, to my eyes, to be further proof. And all in a woman who bore the same name as the girl I had left behind me, that day I went off to war back in old 1862.

So it was not so strange at all, when that moment came at Penn's Landing and I felt the stirring that led me to ask:

"May I kiss you?"

Leigh-the-soldier was not the same as my darling girl. She was not the short, sprightly redheaded firebrand who was my light and who shared my prewar struggles against evil as much as she shared the pleasures of my bedchamber.

Yet on that day, something within me knew that she wasn't a stranger either.

Amazon though she might be, she was anything but an impassive giant. She covered her face with her hands and flushed crimson at my query.

"Forgive me," I said. "Have I . . . have I been too forward?" I was unsure how to interpret her reaction.

"N-no, no . . ." She rearranged the skirt around her legs and slipped closer atop the bench till our knees touched. When she continued, her voice was hushed. "Fuck, I was . . . I swear, you're not gonna believe this, but I was just wishing you'd say something like that."

I leaned closer, my hand alighting atop her knee. The soft fabric of her dress hem and the coarser fibers of her leggings rasped against my palm. "Then shall I interpret that as a yes?"

Oh, but she was a sight in the twilight glow. We were closer still now, forehead to forehead.

"Gods, you're gorgeous." She sighed. "Gods, I just—fuck, kiss me, dammit."

I happily obliged.

Thumb brushing against her lips, my hand cupped the curve of her cheek, and hers grasped my right shoulder. The taste of her was exquisite, even if it was curious for having the metallic notes added by her piercings. An aching yet bemused thought crossed my mind.

It's like the taste of keys. Perhaps I've come home after all.

Of course, I knew it: Leigh-the-soldier was not the

same as the darling girl who had saved me on that long-ago night in Fishtown. And yet . . .

And yet . . . it was her. It had to be.

Everything seemed to hang in blissful stillness when we came up for air at long last: The sound of passing traffic. The whisper of the early summer breeze. The distant hints of conversation from passersby in the park. The cry of seagulls. Leigh's breath, warm on my cheeks. The firmness of her hand at my shoulder. The pounding of my heart in my ears.

"I have no fucking clue what's happening, Chloë," she breathed, "but I love it, and I want more of it, if you do. I'm such shit at hiding it, but gods, deep down, clearer than anything I've felt in a while, I want you. I *want* you."

"Very much." I nodded slowly, a grin warming my cheeks. "You, um . . . yes. I want you too. Very much."

"Want another go?"

It took me a moment to take her meaning, but once I did, I laughed, leaned up until I was half in her lap, and kissed her all over again.

It was heady, and it was addictive, that deep, deep sense of belonging. I think that might have been the first that I truly felt like I might belong in the here and now. There in the park at Penn's Landing, we held each other, and we kissed, and we kissed. Before I knew it, the sun was starting to dip a little lower in the west.

"Wow." She sighed. "Just, wow. I just—fuck, you're amazing."

"Wow, indeed. And plenty more where that came from, darling girl."

She leaned in until our foreheads touched. The curtain of her long, dark hair hung in fragrant waves, tickling my cheek.

"Chloë, I don't understand it. How is it that you fell into my life from out of nowhere, but I feel like . . . like . . ."

"Like what?" I teased with the pad of my thumb, brushing at the piercing below her lip and at the softness of her chin.

"Like I *found* you."

Leigh-the-soldier was not the same as the girl I left behind me all those years ago. Yet my thoughts were a tangled mess at her words.

She was not the same, and yet . . .

"Perhaps there is something to be said for that," I offered. "I certainly am grateful to the Almighty for bringing me to this strange time, if for no other reason than it brought me here and to you."

A momentary shadow crossed her face.

"I dunno if I'd chalk it up to God," she said quietly. "But yeah. Either way, you're here. You're *here*." Just as quickly, she was smiling again. "And um, you're a hella good kisser, you know that?"

I craned my neck and nipped up her chin to her lips.

"Shall we retire somewhere more discreet, then? I should like to show you more of that hidden skill."

"I'd say, 'Carry me to Valhalla, you glorious Valkyrie,' but I'm not gonna make you throw your back out right before a second-stage job interview." She grinned and tapped my chin with an outstretched finger.

"Then we better start walking, darling girl."

"Long as you hold my hand all the way down."

"I may just devour you first."

"*Behave,*" she scolded around a giggle.

We beat a hasty retreat, feet hurrying along, a far cry from the leisurely stroll that had brought us up past Chestnut Street. It was an exquisite sort of torture to go all that way through South Philadelphia, holding hands but wanting to know all of her *now*. We were stealing glances again, as before, but they were unbridled now, hungry.

Somehow, we held ourselves together until we made it all the way back to Federal Street. When we let ourselves in, Hiromi was working at the dining room worktable, poring over her tablet, camera partially disassembled beside her. Her travel suitcase sat in arm's reach, half-emptied.

"*Okaerinasai!*" she called without looking up. "Have a nice walk?"

"*Tadaima!*" I replied. I didn't speak much Japanese back then, but I'd already begun to learn simple household greetings.

When *I* spoke instead of Leigh, she at last looked up.

"Okay, see, see, now I *know* you've been making out." She pointed at us. "Chloë, *you* said *tadaima*—I thought you didn't know any Japanese—and Leigh, *your* lipstick's smudged."

I bit my lip. Leigh tried, and failed, to remain deadpan.

"We're gonna head up." She laughed. "Hold my calls, wouldja?"

"Yeah, yeah." Hiromi shook her head and shooed us away with a sweep of one hand. "*Usero,*" she cackled out in Japanese.

"What's that mean?" I asked as Leigh took me by the hand again and hurried us upstairs.

"Means 'fuck off,'" was her hurried laughing reply.

With the door shut behind us, Leigh pulled me down onto the bed urgently, till we were entangled—her lying back, me perched over her.

"Now, where were we?"

"If I remember correctly, you were complimenting me on my superior skill in matters of kissing."

"Was I now?" she purred. "You'd better refresh my memory, then."

And off we went, kissing with abandon, hands roaming, seeking. It was strange, how familiar it was—the scale was different, of course, the balance between heights changed from before, but in that place beyond words, it was ever the same. It was the same, and I think even she knew it then.

I buried my face in the crook of her neck and nipped with the edge of my teeth.

"F-fuck," she sputtered, pressing against me. "*Fuck*, yeah."

I came up for air. "Is—is that a yes, then, darling girl?"

She wrapped a leg around mine, pulling until she'd brought my thigh between her legs.

"Yes, yes, more, *more.*"

It was a strange sensation, a curious pleasure, to feel her riding my thigh, grinding out a slow rhythm. More familiar was the music of her breath, rising and falling in little gasps and yelps, an old tune on a new instrument.

She wasn't the same, and yet . . .

And yet . . .

So lost were we in each other that only when, at long last, we paused to catch our breath, did I notice the afternoon shadows lengthening outside the windows. Had the time really flown by?

Head pillowed on Leigh's breast, I traced my fingers in little undulating lines around the protective enfolding of her arm.

"An old tune on a new instrument," I murmured.

She shifted. "How's that?"

I looked up at her, up at this woman familiar amid her unfamiliarity. In the sunlight streaming through her drawn blinds, I caught a glimpse of thin, pale scars that ran in crisscrossing lines along the curve of her cheek. Scars that were ordinarily obscured by the hair she wore loose on that side, long and lustrous where the left side was close-cropped around the ear.

I sighed. "You're beautiful, scars and all." I tilted my head back to kiss them, the marks of those years at war. "Even if I haven't seen these particular scars before."

"You make me feel like I can believe it."

My heart ached, but I lingered there, tasting her. Oh, the trembling of her, tension rising and then falling away, melting, melting . . .

"Um, Chloë."

"Hm?"

"Not to be *that* girl," she said, shifting, curling around me, cheek resting against the top of my head. "But we need to be mindful of the time. If we're going to make it to dinner with Mac and Eun-seok, all the way out in Newtown Square, we really should get moving on getting changed."

"What if I devour you first?" I growled against the warm inked expanse of her collarbones and chest.

"Behave." She chuckled. "Your new job isn't official *yet*."

"Is that an order, Sergeant First Class Hunter?"

"You're damn right it is," she purred, kissing my head and then squeezing my backside. "Now, *get*."

"What if I devour you first?" I repeated, clinging to her.

"Hey, now." She laughed. "Save some room for dessert."

TEN

Leigh

*A**hn-nyung! Ban-gab-suum-ne-da!"* ⟨*Hey, good to see you!*⟩
"*Ara maa,*" Pak Eun-seok gasped out in happy
surprise in response to my greeting, adjusting her glasses
and brushing a disheveled lock of hair behind her ear.
"*Yatto kita yo ne, omae wa!*" ⟨*My, 'bout damn time you showed up!*⟩

There was a lot I liked about visiting Brynn and Eun-
seok. There were the safety and company of friends I
trusted, first and foremost—in Brynn's case, a sister in
arms. Then there was the chance to use my Japanese
around someone to whom I'm not related—and to use my
modest extent of Korean as well. Then there was the house
and its surrounding grounds: the joys of a fragrant vege-
table and herb garden, the scent of familiar spices and
home cooking, Korean and Japanese paperbacks stacked
neatly in bookcases beside punk albums and blacksmithing
books and technical manuals, walls with framed art and
photos, fresh catering boxes stacked in boxes and plastic
wrap, 3D printing samples, and other odds and ends scat-
tered in the corners. It was a home that was whole, even in

its disorder. It was something I'd always loved, and something I still kind of aspire to.

One way or another, most importantly, I always felt my gut unclench and my breathing relax when I came up those front steps.

Eun-seok and I exchanged bows, then hugged. "Oh, but I've missed you guys." I smiled. "It really has been a while. Is, ah . . . is Brynn back from work?"

"*Hai, hai.* Cooking already, and she's just about finished too." Eun-seok nodded. "Your timing was frighteningly good. I'm surprised she came back so soon; it sounds like the range was busy today." She half turned and called back into the house, "*Jaghi-ya!* Leigh and Chloë are here!"

After our hurried return from Penn's Landing and getting sidetracked by an eternity of making out and humping, it was a bit of a miracle that we'd gotten ourselves put together and hauled out so quickly.

I gestured to Chloë. "Eun-seok, this is Chloë Stanton. Chloë, this is Pak Eun-seok."

"A pleasure," Chloë replied, dipping into a courtly bow. "Er, um—*Ban-gab-suum-ne-da.*" ⟨*Nice to meet you.*⟩

"The pleasure's mine. It's good to finally meet you."

We followed Eun-seok in, and I wasted no time in making a beeline to the kitchen.

"Evenin', Staff Sarn't! Heard something about white-girl stir-fry happening in the DFAC tonight!" I sang out, sweeping into the kitchen, where Brynn minded a large sizzling wok.

"Yeah, yeah, look what the cat dragged in." She rolled her eyes, acknowledging me with a half tilt of her head and the hint of a smirk. "Hello to you too, Hunter. Make yourself something resembling useful and get me that serving dish over yonder. The brown earthen one—yeah, yeah, that one there. And hold it steady!"

I snorted. "That an order, Staff Sarn't?" I didn't wait for an answer before I brought the dish to the range top, bracing the earthenware on either side, palms steady.

With practiced ease, Brynn picked up the wok and quickly spooned its contents into the waiting dish.

"Psh, asshole," she muttered, gently elbowing me as she finished spooning the stir-fry out with a flourish. Then, all sarcasm gone, she smiled. "Seriously, though, it's good to see you again, Hunter. You're looking . . ." Her voice trailed off as she fished for a word.

"Dressed up fancy?" I offered, with a shift of my hips and a twirl of my sundress.

Brynn shook her head. "Nah. Happy. You look happy."

I heard Chloë step into the kitchen then, and I blushed harder. It was hard to believe: was I really *that* happy after all?

"Chloë, c'mon in," Brynn greeted, wiping a hand clean on her utility skirt before extending it. "Pleasure to finally see you in person."

A moment's hesitation, then Chloë stepped in to take Brynn's hand and shake it firmly. "The honor's mine. Leigh, ah . . . speaks very highly of you."

Brynn turned to smirk sidewise at me. "Hah! I see my terrible reputation precedes me yet again."

"It's not like it's anything you haven't rightfully earned, Mac, after saving my ass a dozen times over—"

"Hey, hey, much as I can't get enough of fulsome praise for all the times you owe me, Hunter," Brynn replied, gesturing at the serving dish in my hands, "be a dear and carry that into the dining room, wouldja?"

"That an order, Staff Sarn't?"

She pointed into the dining room. "Don't make me NJP your ass, Platoon Momma."

"Right on, Staff Sarn't!"

We adjourned to the dining room and took our seats. Chloë looked to me as if for direction and then pulled up a chair to sit beside me, opposite Mac and Eun-seok. Her hand alighted on my thigh, and I swear I could feel the steam already rising out of my ears.

"All right, no reason to stand on ceremony here," Mac urged. "Dig right on in."

We spooned out still sizzling stir-fry and white rice fresh out of the cooker and focused on eating for a while, as anybody in any era might have. For my part, the smell was comforting in its own way, even if it took me back to the bad old days of the Army and being in the closet and being constantly frustrated about where I was in life and where I was headed. There had been many a night where we of Second Platoon staff shared drinks and shitty home-made cooking as we bonded, in the days before that terrible deployment.

"Just like I remember," I remarked, as much to myself as to Mac, as I paused to breathe deeply of the familiar aroma.

"You sure about that?" Mac teased. "The notes of despair and the ambient whiff of horse shit from the farms around Watertown aren't there anymore."

"Why you gotta harsh my vibe, dude?"

She stuck her tongue out at me.

"Love you too, Mac."

I turned to find Chloë contemplating a mouthful, the newness of the flavor clear on her expression.

"What do you think?" I asked.

"It's growing on me." She nodded and took another spoonful. "The seasoning, in particular. I don't think I've ever had anything with quite these notes of flavor before."

"Ginger, seven-spice blend, and sesame oil is some of what you're probably picking up," Mac replied, gesturing to the kitchen over her shoulder with an outstretched thumb. "The sesame oil, in particular, is an old fave."

"Sesame oil." Chloë stared at the still-steaming clumps of shrimp and bamboo shoots in amazement. "Huh. I wouldn't have imagined such a thing. I like it."

"Glad to meet with your approval; not every day I get to cook for someone so recently from uptime. You've got a different appreciation for this stuff, I figure. Flavors ain't what they used to be."

Chloë shook her head and laughed. "You don't know the half of it." She glanced at me, then gestured. "So, if I understand correctly, you and Leigh were together in a platoon of the Fourteenth Infantry. Is everyone at Red Flag a fellow veteran?"

"Not all, but a lot, and not all are American veterans." Eun-seok jabbed a thumb toward her own chest. "I was a KATUSA combat engineer in the ROK Army myself—after I came from the past."

"You are from before as well?" Chloë's eyes were wide.

"From the year 1890."

"And you enlisted?"

"I hadn't transitioned yet, and even people from the past are required to do Army service in Korea."

The *I hadn't transitioned yet* took a moment to land—but then understanding dawned on Chloë's face.

"Two of my closest friends in the old Seventeenth were trans men. They would be pleased to know there are more than a few sisters-in-arms in militaries today."

Eun-seok nodded. "In closet or not, we're more common in armies than a lot of people assume." She shot me a look. "*Sou ja nai, Rii-san?*" ⟨*Isn't that right, Leigh?*⟩

It was true—and I suspect it always will be.

"Yeah—yeah, I guess so!"

Chloë's hand closed again on my thigh. She brushed her thumb against cloth and then gently squeeze. *Not now,* I silently moaned.

"I can see that I'll be in good company," Chloë said.

Mac snorted. "Yeah, well, you'd be even more so if this one got her shit together and joined the crew." She gestured in my direction with the blunt ends of her stainless-steel chopsticks. "A lot of us are vets, but pretty much all of us are queer. Government work makes you miserable anyhow, Hunter. Haven't you had enough?"

"What—hey now, Mac, stay on task, I'm not the one you're vetting for employment here!"

She stuck her tongue out again. "You're cute when you're flustered, Platoon Momma."

"Love you too, Mac . . ."

The banter was light and easy throughout the rest of dinner. Mac and Chloë hashed out the details of her new job. I compared notes with Eun-seok about the recent reading we'd both gotten through. By the time we were done and in the living room, there was soju and coffee out, and while I was keeping my drinking to a very modest extent, I could tell all would be well when Chloë and Mac exchanged shots of soju.

"Welcome to Red Flag Arms, comrade!" Mac crowed. "Here's to success and to queers who take no shit!"

"Hear, hear!" Chloë answered, knocking back the glass with what seemed like practiced ease.

Mac set down her glass. "Now c'mon, let's go get things printed and signed, huh?" She gestured. "My office is that way."

Chloë looked back at me. I worried that she was looking for approval, but instead, I just found that fire again—the one I'd seen in her eyes the day I met her, but more focused, more alive. And just a little bit hungry too—but then, that was hardly a surprise, considering the afternoon's events.

"Go on, make it official." I waved her off. "Go on."

When the two of them headed upstairs, Eun-seok turned to me.

"It will be good for her to have a new face around the range," she said. "Though I know she'd still rather have you there. She's said that from the beginning."

I shook my head. "Chloë needs the job more than I do. I don't matter as much here—"

"Don't say that." Eun-seok frowned. "You matter, and I know you know it."

What could I say? It's easy to say things but harder to actually believe them, especially when you're on-again-off-again dealing with depression wrought by war, bereavement, and trying to figure out what the hell to do with your life after thinking you'd figured it out. I knew, in theory, that she was right, but in my gut, deep down, I'm not sure I really believed it.

"Thanks," I said at last, refilling my coffee cup from the slowly cooling French press. "I could use the reminder from time to time."

"All you have to do is ask Brynn, you know."

"I know." I sighed. "I know."

There it was again, at the back of my head. The memory of what I'd learned, about the commission and why it had come into existence. The guilt the organization bore for having caused this in the first place. I couldn't change it, but I was still part of that organization. Yes, I could leave, but then what?

That was always the question, wasn't it? Then what?

Just like Chloë's, I owed Eun-seok's presence to the temporal rifts my employer had caused. I was grateful to have them both in my life, and I still am. But I couldn't untie that snarled tangle of being employed by the commission but not being happy with my job, wanting to leave but not sure how I'd even do it, and whether or not I could even hold my tongue about the truth. In hindsight, it seems obvious, but at the time, I was still in the thick of it, still lost, unclear and unsure.

I guess it came down to this: I felt I had no right to cut loose now that I was involved with an organization that had caused that kind of massive unseen harm. Why would I deserve anything better?

"You never know," I finally mused. "Life has a way of throwing curveballs. I may just wind up taking Mac up on her offer yet."

"I hope sooner rather than later," was Eun-seok's answer. She gestured with a slight tilt of her coffee cup. "Because Brynn is right, Leigh. Happy looks good on you. And after everything the two of you have been through? You deserve it."

I sat with her words for a little while as I sipped slowly and listened to the sounds of Mac and Chloë's ambient conversation wafting down the stairs. Did I really deserve it, after everything I'd seen and done, not just in the commission but before, in seventen years in the Army? Did I really deserve it?

Chloë soon rejoined us, flopping down beside me, hand slipping around mine and gently squeezing. My heart fluttered.

In hindsight, thinking back to how my heart fluttered and a warm, blissful wave spread to the tips of my toes, I think even then I knew.

Even if I hadn't consciously figured it out yet, I knew: I did indeed deserve better.

I did deserve to be happy.

ELEVEN

Chloë

From the warmth of our reception in Newtown Square, where I was glad to have made new friends and confirmed and cemented the details of my new occupation, we descended West Chester Pike and drove home under the light of a quarter moon. It was July 12. Much of the ride passed in silence. As we crested the little rise to Sixty-Ninth Street and on through Leigh's tiny hometown of Millbourne, she turned to me.

"So yeah, you did it. It's official."

"It is," I replied evenly. "I am at last gainfully employed—and the thought of not having to spin, teach children, or wear a skirt to be gainfully employed appeals to me greatly. Working alongside comrades in arms and comrades in cause, to say nothing of the fact that so many of the people who work there are queer, also appeals to me. I tell you, Leigh, this is good."

She smiled. "Good thing I have you around to remind me of what I take for granted in this day and age."

"My pleasure, darling girl," I purred.

We descended the far slope of the hill out of Mill-bourne and crossed back into the city under the high arches of the elevated rail line at Sixty-Third. At the stoplight, she turned to regard my expression.

"My word," I gasped in wonder.

"Hm?"

"In the city light, surrounded by all that bore you, you look . . . you look gorgeous."

She extended her free hand across the center console, beckoning till I took it in one of mine.

"You know, you'd best be careful there. You keep talking like that, and you know how we're gonna end up."

"How's that?" I queried.

"With my head between your legs, drinkin' deep."

My heart leaped.

"I think I could get used to that." I laughed. "Unless I devour you first."

"Now, now, remember what I told you before we headed out."

"I know, darling girl, I know." I smirked. "*Behave*. But you know well and good enough by now that I am hardly one to always follow the rules."

The light turned green, and she drove on, eyes back on the road but the rest of her clearly elsewhere.

"Is that a threat, Sergeant Stanton?"

"Maybe," I growled. "Let's see where it takes us."

Through the streets of West Philadelphia, still lively at so late an hour, we passed from the shadow of the elevated rail out into University City. Ahead of us lay the stately white columns of the Thirtieth Street Station and the glittering towers of Center City above, waiting beyond on the Schuylkill's far bank.

"The skyscrapers." I squeezed Leigh's hand. "It's

funny. They amazed me that first day. Now they're just a fact of life, part of the new tapestry that is my every day. Like another giant I know."

"*Behave.*" She giggled. "I'm still driving."

"Of course, of course."

The streets at this late hour were, for the most part, quite empty. Weaving around City Hall, we wound southward, ever southward, down into South Philadelphia and Passyunk Square. When at last we pulled in on Federal Street, a short walk from the house, I let go of her hand and undid my seat harness.

"Home again," I murmured. I turned to find Leigh looking at me again, her eyes clearly misty.

"What's the matter, darling girl?"

She shook her head. "Nothin'. Just that I don't think anybody's ever said that about anywhere I've lived before."

I shifted in my seat, leaned over the center console till I was cupping her cheek, and brushed the curve of her chin. Her cheeks were warm.

"May I kiss you?" I asked her again.

"*Please,*" she breathed.

We kissed and kissed, until at long last she stopped me when we came up for air, a finger to my lips.

"Let's do this inside, huh? Bed and everything."

"O-oh," I sputtered. "Y-yes, yes, of course."

We locked up the car and hurried to the house. Hiromi was nowhere in sight, so we forewent the usual household greetings, discarded our footwear by the door, and then hurried up the stairs. In Leigh's bedroom again, I loosened my necktie, undid the top button of my blouse, and dropped to the softness of her bed and the stuffed toys that lined its plush, dark-blue covers.

"All right," she declared. "Before we go any further,

gimme a sec. There's something I need to do first, before anything else."

Rounding the bed, she recovered the little laptop computer that sat on the carpet beneath one of the tall windows. With practiced ease, she lowered herself to the carpet, stretched, and switched on the machine. In a moment, she was swiping about on its capacitive screen, and typing hurriedly.

"What's the matter?" I asked, as I undid a couple more buttons of my blouse.

"Hold that thought," she commanded, one hand raised in caution, her eyes still on the screen. "Hold that thought, hold that thought . . ."

"Honestly, what's—"

"Okay!" she proclaimed triumphantly. Then she looked up at me, beaming. "There!"

I cocked my head. "What happened?"

"*That*, retired Sergeant Chloë Parker Stanton, was the email by which my professional responsibility for you officially ends." She shut the laptop and set it down, rose, and practically pounced onto the bed. "If we're going to be doing anything further that involves this bed and various states of undress, we can do it now without worrying about what some fucking federal government desk jockey at the office under the Moyamensing Institute or at headquarters in DC is gonna say."

I slipped my other leg onto the bed till I was sitting cross-legged, all the while looking down at her pleased, triumphant smile.

"So that means—"

"Yours," she purred. "All yours."

Words fell away as we kissed. Softly at first, almost hesitantly, but growing slowly more intense, tongues probing deeper, ever deeper. I leaned in, hand cupping her cheek, leaning lower and lower till I lost my balance and collapsed onto her, gasping for breath.

Limbs tangled, we laughed at the joyous awkwardness of it.

Again, I found myself thinking it. *A new, different instrument, but a familiar tune.* This was familiar. I'd been here before.

She rearranged herself, shimmying, and tugged the dress up past her shoulders and off, discarding it on the carpet beside the bed. I unbuttoned the rest of my blouse, loosened and cast aside my tie, and now we sat in our underwear from the waist up—she in leggings, I in my trousers.

I hooked my arm around her, fingers caressing, seeking, tracing a meandering web of paths up and down till they arrived at the small of her back, probing, scratching, *needing*. Planting a hand beside me for balance, I let myself untense. Deep down in my gut, I knew: I *wanted* her. *Needed* her.

A moan rose to my lips, one that seemed to well up from my core, up and up until it was smothered against her lips. First one and then the other, I uncrossed my legs and scooted up until I was higher and steadier. We hung on and kept probing, kept kissing, kept seeking with our hands, neither of us letting go until we fell away gasping for air, lungs burning and cheeks flushed. I reached out to caress her cheek, my fingers brushing back her bangs. The fire in her eyes was consuming, electric.

"Oh, Leigh Andrea Hunter, you are perfect." I turned my head, leaning closer to brush my lips against her cheeks. "You are perfect. You are . . . *magnificent*. And I want you."

Beneath my hands, she shivered.

"Yours," she breathed. "Oh, Chloë, I am *yours*, all *yours*." Then, regaining a measure of energy, she sat up till she was looking down at me and gave me a fang-baring grin. "Now, what were you saying a while ago about devouring?"

I tapped a finger against her forehead and slowly traced a lazy line down the bridge of her nose and on, till it brushed her lips.

"*Yes.*" The clarity in that one little word scared me just a bit, but it was so plain, and I knew as well as she did that I meant it. "*Yes.*"

I straddled her and drew my nails over her shoulder to follow the line of her neck up to the shorter side of her undercut, reaching in, drinking every little note of pleased breath and yelp that came from her. Leigh's hands wandered my back, clawing haphazardly and shifting to support my weight as I leaned further into her lap.

She pressed against me. "Yes! Yes!" she squeaked as I kissed my way along her cheek, nipping at her earlobe, teasing at her industrial piercing. The small hairs on her neck stood on end.

Her voice rose, pinched, almost pleading. "Please, oh please! Yes, more! Ahh, fuck, *more!*"

I shifted in response to that. My right hand brushed up, up, up, nails scratching and tickling at the short hairs of her undercut before I weaved my fingers farther up through her hair, stroking in little circles. Above her, triumphant, I lingered. From all she'd said and shown, I could afford to take my time and tease.

Her eyes went unfocused, breath a little ragged. "Please, please, please, oh gods, please—"

I cocked my head in an overdramatized pantomime of deep thought. "Hmm . . . more, then?" My right hand still moved in little circles atop her head, while my left hand teased at the back of her neck.

Once, twice, three times, she nodded, trembling hands reaching up and fumbling at my chest. "Oh, fuck yes, more, more, please, gods yes."

I drank it in. I lingered, savoring the need in her eyes as I tugged off my bra and cast it aside. Then I returned and began working my way down from her cheek to her neck, and farther south, planting kisses and gentle love bites to mark my path all the way down.

She made a little moan that was positively delicious.

"That good, was it?" I chuckled. "High praise, darling girl."

"Y-yuhuhhh . . ."

Probing with the tips of my fingers, I found the crotch of her leggings positively damp. Deftly, I reached around behind her to unhook her bra. Then I pulled a breast free, my fingers alternately pinching and brushing circles around a nipple that already stood at attention.

"Glad to see I meet with your approval," I cooed, sliding lower till I could take the waiting rosy nipple into my mouth. I gently suckled, one hand cupped around the breast's soft outer curve. Pausing, I looked up to make eye contact, her breast still in my mouth, just a hint of teeth sharp against the nipple and its piercing. She met my gaze through swimming, hazy eyes, and again she quivered beneath me and cried out, a note that was long and ecstatic. With my eyes still on hers, I tugged slightly with my teeth, and she bucked, fingers clawing at my back, legs gone to jelly. Slowly, steadily, I bit, tugged, squeezed, and sucked, trying my best to toe the line between just enough and too much.

After a while, as I kissed and licked my way up to her

neck, she shifted, hooking her legs around one of mine as she'd done before, pulling it closer, between her thighs, tight, and eagerly ground against my thigh. She buried her face in the crook of my neck, fairly wailing against me as she ground her way to a higher pitch. I rearranged myself, holding her close, holding her against me, our breasts pressed together, hardened nipple brushing hardened nipple, urged on by each other's touch.

"Come for me, Leigh. Come for me, come on—you're close, you're so close. Come for me."

The wave crested, and she came with a high, desperate cry of exultation. Shaking, shaking, and then slowly going slack, she melted into me, spent and still.

It took me a moment to realize there were tears on my cheeks along with the sweat. They were, I knew, tears of relief. Hadn't the girl I'd left behind me trembled and ground and keened beneath me like this too?

I petted Leigh's hair, rocking her slowly as she lay against me.

"Yes, that's it. That's it. Good girl." She trembled, and I thought she was trying to say something, but instead, she simply sighed and stayed still, the rhythm of her breath slowly settling.

"Magnificent," I murmured. "Oh, but you are *magnificent*, darling girl."

"Wow," she rasped at last, cheek still nestled against the crook of my neck. "Just, fucking *wow*."

"Wow, indeed." I laughed. "And plenty more where that came from."

She let out a happy little squeak at that. But for the longest time, she just stayed there, spent, loose, and warm against me.

"Chloë, I can't remember the last time. The last time I

felt this way after sex. Warm. Content. *Happy.* I can just be me. I can just be here." She turned her head and kissed at the slope of my jaw. "I can just be enough."

"You are enough," I affirmed.

I looked down at her, at *my* girl, beaming with joy, pride, and a lingering hint of lust in her eyes. She'd recovered enough to flop over, rest her head on a pillowing arm, and look up at me with a playful smirk.

"My dear Sergeant Stanton. Something has occurred to me. Do you realize what this all means?"

"Hmm? And what's that, Sergeant First Class Hunter?"

"It's the damnedest thing, if you think about it. I guess for once, the infantry came first!"

She laughed, then I laughed. I flopped onto the mattress beside her, gasping for air amid our shared merriment.

"Combined-arms pillow talk. I thought I'd seen it all, but I think combined-arms pillow talk is a first for me."

"Well, I am glad to keep surprising you." She smiled and stroked my cheek with the back of her hand.

We lay there for a while, still content, still taking in the peace and warmth of each other's presence after our earlier foray. When she shifted and the curtain of her long, lustrous hair revealed her right cheek, my breath hitched.

"What's the matter?" she asked, voice gentle, and shifted closer to lay a hand on my thigh.

"You know," I said, "it just occurred to me, this might be the first time I've seen so many of your scars."

We sat up, rearranging ourselves. She shrugged off her undone bra, and we sat kneecap to kneecap in the soft lamplight. A blush tinged her cheeks.

"I think this might be the first time I've seen so many of yours," she replied, gesturing to my arms.

I could feel a blush tinging my cheeks in turn. I hadn't even thought of that. That I felt this much at ease, to the point that I hadn't even given a second thought to whether she'd see them—she *really* wasn't just anybody at all.

She took one of my hands in hers and slowly, reverently, guided it over her scars.

Her cheek, skin soft but uneven with the marks of her brush with death on that day she saw the Divine on the battlefield. "Syria. Battle of Jisr Ibrahim."

A constellation of pockmarks, some wide and thick, mostly hidden among the sleeve tattoo covering her right arm. "Also Jisr Ibrahim." Farther down, a pair of long lines on her forearm, beneath the tattoo of roses that covered it from elbow to wrist. "Hand-to-hand fighting in Al-Najaf in 2003."

On her left arm, another cluster of thick, jagged scars obscured by the crest of her old division. "A bad fucking day in Korengal Valley in 2011."

Then, with her hand still wrapped around mine, she cupped my cheek and drew me into another long, lingering kiss.

"You're beautiful," I said, my eyes swimming with tears. "You're beautiful, scars and all."

"You make me feel like maybe, just maybe, I can believe it."

My heart ached with her words, even as it still soared for this new direction our relationship had begun to take.

The moment was right. Taking her hand as she'd taken mine, I brought it to my left upper arm and the thick, roughly parallel lines that were the last mark of a long-dead surgeon.

"It seems right to do for you as you've done for me," I reassured her. "This was Chancellorsville. I got lucky. Only the one bullet went clean through, and thank God it did not break any bones. Bullets just grazed me the other two times."

My scars aren't nearly as numerous as hers, and her history at war is far longer than my own. Weaponry in the present has, from all I've seen, grown significantly more fearsome. Yet war remains as it ever was, in the most fundamental ways. Of this we'd shared our memories in the time we'd come to know each other—a bridge of pain to which we'd added newer peaceful, beautiful things—and now we were here, skin to skin.

She was hushed, her expression aghast. "*Grazed?*" she mouthed. "Fuck, this looks like it might've—"

"*Grazed*, aye," I repeated, clenching and unclenching my free left hand. "Well, compared to what others got, anyway. It still stings, but I live with it. Lordy, I was scared, though—they could've found me out in the surgeon's tent, but thank God they didn't. By some miracle, I made it back to my regiment."

She bit her lip and nodded. "That sounds like neuropathy, by the way. There are things you can do for that now."

"I'll remember," I replied. Then, switching hands, I guided hers to my right shoulder and spots on the upper arm. "Brandy Station." The scars were thick and uneven. A few were short, but the longest traced a line all the way from my shoulder to the top of my breast. "That Reb's saber had to cut through a good three layers of clothing, but I still got scraped pretty bad. Stung for a week, but I didn't tell anybody. And I still have burns on my hands too." I offered her one palm, outstretched. "Turns out, there isn't much other option for unjamming a half-molten

Smith round when your carbine jams than pulling it out by hand. Damned infernal rubber rounds."

Gently, she closed both hands around mine and held them to her chest. "And I thought *I* had small-arms problems." She chuckled softly, even as she blinked back tears to meet my gaze. "*I* never had to fucking unjam molten rubber out of my M110 or M4 barehanded."

"You were fortunate," I offered, "as much as any of us at war could be. Good *lord* that stung."

A moment's silence. Our fingers parted but soon found each other again in my lap. Almost hesitantly, Leigh spoke.

"Chloë, listen. I . . . I still don't know if I can explain what *this* is, what's happening between us, but it feels good and right, and I want it, more of it, if you do."

I stretched forward to kiss her.

"Yes, *yes*," I breathed, moving closer still, until the softness of her full breasts pressed against mine. "Yes, I want it too."

We kissed again, deeper, her tongue probing my mouth and her fingers brushing through my hair. Her piercings were cool points where they brushed my skin. This close, her scent was clearer—a hint of leather, old books, and grass.

Leigh smiled coyly once we'd parted for breath. "I think it's time the cavalry came." She snaked a finger from my collarbone down, till it halted between my breasts. "Unsupported infantry don't do too well even today, y'know."

I grinned. "What's your strategy, then?"

"I'll keep you abreast." She smirked, sliding slowly to the floor as she kissed along the curve of my breast. At last, she took a nipple between her lips and sucked slowly, tenderly.

"*Oh,*" I gasped out, even as I groaned at her punning. "Oh, that . . . *oh, my* . . . that was right terrible." Snaking a hand up to cradle her head, I gently petted as she expertly nipped and sucked. "Mm, good girl." She subtly shivered, and when she looked up, the hunger was clear in her eyes.

She grinned. "So what do you think, hmm? Am I good enough to keep going?"

"Good enough?" I bit my lip. "You're magnificent, darling girl."

Brushing a stray lock of hair from her eyes, she returned her attention lower, suckling one breast while circling the other nipple with the pad of her thumb in a slowly growing rhythm. I shifted, wrapping one leg and then the other around her, leaning forward as I did. One hand to the mattress, I cradled her head with the other, fumbling for purchase as I threaded my fingers through her long locks and felt the short, shaven sides rasping against the heel of my palm. She worked her way slowly downward, too preoccupied now with teasing the thin, downy hairs and subtly plush curve of my belly below my navel to care about anything else.

"Perfect . . . you're perfect . . . oh, you're . . ." A shiver raced through me. "*Yes!*"

She paused again to look up at me through hair unbound and eyes full of need and hunger. "I want to taste you," she breathed, fingers resting at the waistband of my black denim. I caught her meaning, but from the beginning, I had already known what I wanted.

"Silly girl, *take me,*" I instructed between breaths gone ragged. "*Take me.*"

Her lips seemed to linger at every inch that came bare

behind another undone button of the fly, warm through the fabric of my boxers. My need was building, and her slow going only drove me wilder.

"Mm, you're so fucking wet," she purred approvingly, slipping a finger under the waistband of my boxers now, exquisitely close and still excruciatingly far. "Nice to know the feeling is mutual."

I bit my lip again as she traced a wet line with her tongue while the boxers came down. Finally, she spread me with deftly placed fingers and dutifully buried her face in my crotch.

"*There,*" I hissed, toes curling as the wave of wet warmth built within me. I could feel her softly humming against my clitoris. "*There*, yes, right *there* . . . don't stop now, Leigh, don't stop now . . ."

It turned into a blur then, with little clear but her mouth on my antipodes and my voice distantly calling her name and the wave of inner fire that carried me into a blissful near oblivion. At last, the wave crested, and I came hard, tears of relief further blurring my vision as I trembled and gradually went slack against her. We lay there for a long time.

Finally, she scooted closer, grunting as she shifted, before she leaned in to kiss the curve of my belly, lips still slick with my warm wetness from moments before. Hand still subtly trembling, I reached out to slowly pet her now thoroughly disheveled hair.

"Hey." Her voice was hushed and so very small. "How'd I do?"

I sat up and laid her head in my lap. "Oh, my good girl, you're perfect." I sighed, stroking her unkempt mane of raven black with the back of my hand as I trailed a lone finger through it. "Leigh Andrea Hunter, you are *perfect.*

And I will personally have the hide of anybody, either side of Mason-Dixon, who says otherwise."

For a while, she said nothing, simply nestling closer, hands resting inside the open circle of my legs, more utterly spent than I was. What was she thinking, I wondered. Was she getting lost in thought again, in the weight of her past and mine and the strange force that seemed to draw us inexorably to each other? I didn't know. After a moment, she sighed, rearranged herself more comfortably, and laid a hand on my thigh.

"Thank you," she said simply. I could hear the edge of tears in her voice, but there was a gentle smile on her face. "*Thank* you."

Upon her urging, we headed for the shower soon afterward, our bodies having borne so thoroughly the marks of such fortunate though unanticipated consummation. Leigh and I made small talk for a little while as we bathed and dressed, but eventually, the scope of it began to sink in, and we passed into a stunned yet happy silence.

We changed into nightclothes—I donned a loose flannel and my boxers, she fresh leggings and her oversized hooded Army sweater—and we wandered down to the kitchen to snack and enjoy the quiet of the house and the comfort of each other's company.

"I'm curious," she finally asked as she munched, passing me the little tin of mixed fruits and nuts. In the darkened kitchen, her voice was hushed. "How did you know? I mean, about me and you. And all this. And . . . my feelings for you."

I cocked my head for a moment to mull it over, then simply shook my head. "Honestly? I don't know if I *knew* before today. But a gut feeling? Yes, ma'am, *definitely*."

I picked at some cashews. I wanted to tell her then and there: *It's you. It has to be you. An old melody on a new instrument, but it's you.*

"I felt," I said at last, "that I could take a leap of faith."

Her cheeks flushed.

"Honestly, Chloë, I think I've had a crush on you for a while. But when you asked me at Penn's Landing today, I . . . I guess I felt like I could take my own leap of faith too. And now here we are, having late-night postcoital trail mix and seltzer in my kitchen."

I laughed. "Indeed. And thank goodness for that."

Yes. *Yes.* This was good. This was right. Then and there, in my heart, I decided. Whatever the truth was of the tie between this Leigh and the one I remembered, this woman would have all of me.

TWELVE

Leigh

It was heaven, that first night Chloë and I were together. It was heaven, and when we fell asleep, it was blissful, deep oblivion.

I forgot where I was for a surprisingly long time when I started to wake up the morning after that amazing first night with her. My world had turned upside down, and everything felt new. It was as though I were looking at everything around me with new eyes. All I knew, as I woke up the morning after with Chloë tucked inside the curl of my arm and legs as the little spoon, was that I felt light, and while I couldn't remember the dreams I'd had, I was certain that I had slept well.

Happy, Mac had said. *You look happy.*

You deserve to be happy, Eun-seok had said.

And you know? I think I honestly felt it, for real and without any reservations or qualifiers. It was as though I were back after a long, long trip away—back here, back beside her. Back where I belonged.

I still didn't get it; I still didn't know why I felt that

way or what business I had feeling that way. But it was a fact, and I loved it. Without anything urgent to do that morning, I just let it sit. I let myself lie there and drink in her warmth; the feeling of the sun on my cheeks as it came through the blinds; the cool air against the bare skin at the small of my back, where my hoodie had ridden up; and the thousand and one little sounds of the house around me and the ambient notes of the streetscape beyond the windows.

In a word, that morning was *perfect*.

After a while, I felt Chloë stir, felt her shift inside my arms. She turned her head and nuzzled it against my chest.

"Morning." She yawned. "It's warm here."

"Hey, gorgeous." I smiled. "You're one hell of a reveille. Good morning."

She laughed, yawned again, and burrowed back deeper against me.

"It's nice to wake up next to someone for a change," I felt, as much as heard, her murmur. "I like sleeping among books without a doubt, but this is so much nicer. So much warmer." She nipped the inside of my arm, and I yelped in surprise, though not unpleasantly so. "So much softer too."

"Right back atcha." I giggled. "I can't remember the last time it wasn't just me here. It's nicer this way."

"That's quite the surprise to me, darling girl," she growled. She stretched a leg out to curl around mine and slowly rubbed at the back of my leg with the gentle rasp of a socked foot. "I'd have thought you'd have all manner of women practically begging for you to be theirs. You're strong, brilliant, beautiful. Quite the catch."

She wasn't the first person to tell me that.

"Never really went anywhere. Besides, before transition, I was dating straight girls and clearly wasn't what they were looking for, and ever since transition, I've always had to deal with not meeting a whole other set of expecta-tions." I buried my nose in the messy waves of her auburn hair. "Apparently, having been a soldier means I'm sup-posed to take the lead in everything. *Everything.*"

Chloë shifted beneath me. "That doesn't sound like a recipe for happiness."

"Yeah, not really. Not at all."

Had any of my relationships, regardless of duration, regardless of pre- or post-transition, ever been satisfying? Had they ever felt truly safe? Had I ever had my guard down all the way, like I did now?

"Lucky me, though," I added. "Lucky me."

In hindsight, it's so obvious—all of it. But at the time, all I could think as I lay there was just that. *Lucky me.*

We wandered down to the kitchen after a while. Even cozy feels have no power over hunger pangs when the nearest food is three floors down. We set to work making breakfast. I was cooking waffles, while Chloë cautiously babysat the espresso pot, when Hiromi came down the stairs, dressed for work. She paused in the kitchen doorway and looked from me to Chloë and back again.

She tried to keep a straight face as she arched an eye-brow, but I could hear the laughter in her words. *"Me ga kirakira shite mabushii."* ⟨*Your eyes are sparkling so hard, it's blinding.*⟩ Then, in English, "Suspicious, very suspicious."

"Good morning, sunshine," I sang out. "Waffles and shenanigans afoot!"

"No shit." She smirked, making for the fridge. Leaning in, she furrowed her brow for a moment before retrieving a brown paper bag with her lunch for the day. "I had an inkling of it last night, I think."

There was that metaphorical steam-coming-out-my-ears feeling again.

Chloë sputtered. "Hiromi, I really must apologize. I, that is we—"

"Relax, girl scout, relax." Hiromi laughed, gesturing for Chloë to calm. "Relax and keep an eye on the coffeepot."

"Surely we must have caused offense—"

"Psh, relax. The house's walls don't always insulate sound well, but it isn't anything I haven't heard before. On top of that, I was kinda waiting for this to happen. Kinda surprised it hadn't already."

Chloë glanced up at me. "Really?"

"Serious pent-up Big Lesbian Energy going on here for a while now." Hiromi gestured between us. "Now gangway! Lemme at the coffee machine."

She passed between us to retrieve the carafe from the quietly hissing coffee machine.

"Seriously, though," she said as she poured herself a travel mug. "It's about damn time. Though, Leigh, I guess that means *you* have to head back to work as usual pretty soon?"

My heart sank. I'd quite forgotten since the night before.

"Um, yeah. Yeah, I guess I do. Huh." I turned back to minding the waffle iron. "Gotta get back to the grind. Tomorrow, I think—go back, reclaim my desk, and all that office bitch shit."

There was a moment of tense silence.

"Fun times," she quipped. "Embracing the suck."

"Yeah, yeah . . ."

"Well, I'm off," Hiromi declared. "Don't burn the house down with the flames of all that pent-up lovemaking now, ya hear?"

"Yeah, yeah." I rolled my eyes.

"Chloë, we still on for round two of photo drone flight training?"

"Ready whenever you are."

Hiromi turned, fiddled with her bag, and then hefted it with a grunt.

"*Ittekimasu.*" ⟨*I'll be off now.*⟩

"*Itterasshai.*" ⟨*See you when you get back.*⟩ The Japanese word still sounded a little unwieldy coming from Chloë's lips.

After the door thudded shut, I let myself exhale. For a little while longer, I'd averted an impossible conversation.

"You're getting better there," I remarked as I poured some more waffle batter into the iron. "With the Japanese, I mean."

The coffeepot hissed and burbled. Chloë fumbled with the knob but managed to switch off the gas range in short order.

"Am I really?"

"Yeah. But remember, an *i* is pronounced 'ee.' 'Ee-teh-rah-shah-ee.'"

"*Itterashai,*" she said slowly. "Hm. I shall try to remember that."

I scraped out the final round of waffles. "Good. You're learning quick."

"I'd like to learn it, darling girl," she said, pouring one mug and then another. "It's your other language."

"One of them." I nodded, warming my hands around one of the mugs. "But it's the one I grew up with at home, aside from English."

"At any rate . . ." She smirked. "One more language for me to woo you in."

"Psh. I can see I'm in trouble."

"Right you are."

162

We adjourned to the table in the common room with dishes and mugs and breakfasted in the late-morning sun. After a while, I put on some music and went back to the kitchen for a refill from the coffee machine.

"I just realized," Chloë observed on my return, gesturing at the low bookcases against the far wall. "That's a bow sitting on top of the bookshelves, isn't it?"

"Hm? Oh. Oh, yeah. Yeah, that's a bow." I heaved a long, deflating sigh. I had to do this right. *Fuck, this crosses back into shit I don't want to talk about . . .*

I sat back down but turned to look the bow over as I explained.

"It's a family heirloom. My great-great-great-grandfather, Mitsuya Toshikuni, carried this bow to war."

"What war was he in?

"The Boshin War—er, the Japanese version of the War of Rebellion, but in that war, the north—northern Japan, that is—lost."

"Did they all use bows?"

"Not all. His overlord, Date Yoshikuni of Sendai, had an army that used bows, swords, Enfield rifles, and Gatling guns, all at once."

Chloë nodded slowly. "Makes sense to use what's already at your disposal in a war, especially a war of insurrection."

I sipped at my refilled coffee, then dunked a waffle in it to nibble at.

"The bow has been passed down in my family since then. I'm one of the first two since him to take up archery and the first to go to war. And now it's mine."

"You use the same bow?"

"No—no, not at all." I shook my head. "I've got my own gear, courtesy of one of my aunts in Japan."

"Does it—can this one still be used, then?"

"Oh, it can, it can." I finished the last little bit of waffle. "I just don't feel like I can use it."

"Why's that?"

I wanted to tell her. I wanted to tell her all of it, just then. I'd have squared my shoulders, turned to look her in the eye, and said it all:

The commission's predecessor organization fucked with the flow of space-time to change history to be more advantageous to the United States. They picked a target to change and chose the Boshin War. History wasn't supposed to be like this, but now it is, and we have to live with it. The Boshin War, the Second World War, the Cold War—that's how it is now, and there are holes in history, and we don't know when or if they can be sealed. Why would I fucking deserve to use this bow? I'm part of the organization that's the reason my ancestor and his kinfolk lost a war he should've had a hand in winning.

"Too much pressure," I finally said. "I was the first Mitsuya in one hundred fifty years to go to war and the second in the same time to even bother taking up a bow at all. I've got family on both sides of the Pacific who feel pretty damn strongly about that. Besides, say I did use that bow—what if I broke it? I'd have cousins from here all the way to Natori lining up to have my neck."

Slowly, she set down her mug and squinted in contemplation, eyeing me, then the bow, then me again.

I could practically hear her saying it: *Lying doesn't become you, darling girl.*

"What if you did it justice, though?"

"Huh?"

"What if you do justice to your ancestor's legacy?"

My cheeks burned. *What if, indeed.*

"I . . . honestly, I don't know," I admitted. "Maybe that's something to work on."

"I look forward to it," was her quiet reply. "In the meanwhile, perhaps I may see your skill with the bow sometime?"

"My archery gear is in the closet on the second floor. Been a little while since I put in some range time with my bow, but maybe that can be arranged."

She rose, rounded the table, and looked a little closer at the bow. "You know, for that matter, I don't think I've seen your shooting skill with a rifle yet, either."

I perked up a bit. "Is that a challenge?"

She cocked an eyebrow and came to sit beside me on the bench. "Would you like it to be?"

"The Army didn't even do marksmanship training in your time." I smirked. "Are you sure you could handle it?"

"Why, we were too busy sharpening our skill in the field," she retorted, leaning in to brush my cheek with the back of her hand. "That kind of sharp eye honed in action is irreplaceable."

"Ooh, I can see you've got me lined up for a perfect shot. I'm in trouble."

We kissed, with her leaning halfway into my lap, an awkward, happy tangle of limbs.

"You're darned right you are."

The echoes of all I'd left unsaid still hung in the background like smoke that refused to clear. Sooner or later, I knew I would have to deal with it. But for then and there, all I knew was the relief. Something inside me, deep and very old, seemed to whisper to me in the little quiet spaces.

Home, it seemed to say. *I'm home.*

THIRTEEN

Chloë

They have a saying in this time: *I smell bullshit.* I don't know when exactly I first smelled it coming from Leigh, but the closer we grew, the more it seemed obvious that she was talking around something, and that it wasn't really something *small.*

Those of us who have been to war have seen the proverbial elephant and have had to do things to survive that we might've blanched at before. We have our share of these things in life; this much I'll grant. But it wasn't about that, as far as I could tell. It didn't manifest at times when she was talking about her time in the Army. It was something different, I knew, but *what* it was wasn't clear to me.

Of course, at the beginning—once she'd sent in the papers and rendered me free of the commission's oversight—there was plenty to celebrate, and there was plenty else that held my attention. To be fair, there was plenty else on my mind when it came to this new state of affairs with Leigh-the-soldier.

In this new time, there were any number of new terms

that one could use to describe the dynamic we now had. The queer women I met through Leigh and Hiromi's local connections seemed to favor quite a few different ones, both terms for one's significant other and pet names. *Girlfriend* now had a romantic connotation to which I was a novice. *Partner* was one I often heard, sometimes used in reference to a spouse.

As we settled into the new dynamic, we did not hurry to call it anything, at least not for a little while. It was enough to just let it be what it was, to enjoy it, and to see where it took us. But eventually, it was Leigh who first said it, one day when we were chatting with some of her local acquaintances at the Silver Bullet. In a voice tinged with deep and certain pride, she introduced me as "my girlfriend, Chloë."

I guess the surprise was writ plainly across my face. She noticed and was momentarily aghast.

"Oh, shit, I'm sorry. We still hadn't worked out what to call—"

"No, no." I shook my head. "I like it. It feels good to the ears and to the heart."

So. *Girlfriend* became the term we used for each other. And it felt good. Very good.

But the shadow of all I knew had been left unsaid, on both our parts, seemed to follow behind us, despite the happiness and light. As she returned to her job at the commission and I began mine at Red Flag Arms in Broomall, it continued to quietly nag at me.

Red Flag was, and is, a good place to work. The commute was a bit of a challenge at the outset: I didn't have my driving license at that point and had to be driven out either by Leigh or Hiromi from Passyunk Square or by Eun-seok coming to get me from Newtown Square. Many of the em-

ployees there, like Brynn, Eun-seok, and I, were veterans—
though apart from Eun-seok, I was the only temporally displaced person who worked there. And just as Eun-seok
had observed, almost all of us were queer of some kind or
another. The resulting dynamic was lively, collegial, and
somewhat surprisingly to my eyes, *fun.*

What was more of a surprise, and a pleasant one at
that, was the political currents of those who worked there,
and of the establishment as a whole. Leigh had been clear
on Brynn and Eun-seok's leanings, but they weren't alone.
There were activists and community organizers among my
new colleagues. It was in the name—Red Flag—and like
Leigh had told me at the outset, that was not coincidental
and was, indeed, a tribute to the revolutionaries of 1848.

I was still catching up on the causes of the day and the
language through which modern politics was parsed and
fought. Regardless, I grew to recognize and appreciate that
this was a place of action and these were people of action.
And Red Flag's major mission was teaching practical skills
to minorities like mine in the interest of improving their
common defense and broader betterment, as well as the
usual business of sale of equipment, instruction, and weaponry, as desired.

It was large too: a massive split-level affair housed in
the shell of an old supermarket. At the beginning, I
could've sworn I would get lost in it. But in time, I grew
acclimated, and navigating it became second nature.

One of my favorite places to sit when I was having
lunch pretty quickly became one of the second-floor meeting rooms that overlooked the bay where an artificial wall
simulated a rock face. I'd sit, sup, and contemplate that
craggy face and the occasional client scrabbling up it like a
mountain goat.

It was during one of those lunchtimes in late August that Brynn found me there.

"Admiring the view, Stanton?"

"Something like that." I gestured to the seats ringing the conference table behind me. "Please, feel free to sit, if you'd like. I'm going to head back in a few minutes."

She settled into one of the chairs. In her hands was a dented old travel mug. I smiled to myself as I recognized the crossed-bayonet crest I'd come to know so well.

"That's the Tenth Mountain's crest."

"A memento," she remarked, lifting the mug to look at the crest. "It sucked, but the people who were with me through it were what made it any good."

I thought of Caldwell and Nate. "I feel the same about my regiment and war. A terrible war, but on the whole, I fought alongside some right fine people."

"Speaking of," she said, taking another drag at the mug, "how are things going with Hunter?"

Now that was the question, wasn't it?

"Doing fine, doing fine," I answered briskly as I finished off the last of my pork bao buns. "Settling into the new state of things, now that we're together and both back to our respective places of work."

It was true, sure, but it wasn't everything. That cloud of uncertainty still followed me.

"She's a stubborn dumbass sometimes, but she's my sister by choice, and I love her to death," Brynn replied. "It's nice to see her happier than I've seen her in a good long while."

"Was she unhappy?"

Brynn sat back and put her feet up on the table. "Honestly? With that government job she's got, I think she still is. Until you showed up, she hid it a little better, but even then, it was kinda plain. Everybody likes to bitch about how their job is terrible, but I think working for the commission eats away at her in a way not even the Army did."

I turned in my chair. "You can see it too, then."

"Yeah. It's like it weighs on her. I keep telling her, I'm *dying* to get her over here, but even if it wasn't here, I think she'd actually thrive if she were anywhere else. Sometimes I think she's maybe seen some shit that she can't tell anyone and that it weighs on her that way. And yeah, sure, she's probably had to sign a dozen nondisclosure forms, but seriously, sometimes it reminds me of how she was right before she came out. The weight of everything she was keeping to herself kind of . . . it was plain, and when she actually did something about it, the change was palpable."

I thought it over, thought of everything I'd seen since I met her: the big and the little things I'd gotten to know about Leigh and her relationship with her job.

"It has seemed to me, sometimes, like there is something . . . something on the tip of her tongue that she can't bring herself to say." I nodded, rising to stretch. "What that is, I can't begin to speculate. Besides, I'm not entirely sure what's within my means to do, to probe and gain some further measure of insight as to what might be the matter."

Brynn shrugged. "It's not exactly the same kind of situation, but I figure the best thing to do is what I did in the time before she worked up the nerve to deal with being in the closet in any real way. You aren't gonna force it out of her; you just gotta be there to catch her when she makes that leap. Or trips and falls."

"Brynn, I have to say, it's difficult to live with." I shook my head. "Lying doesn't become her, and it bothers me to know there's something she feels she has to hold back like that."

"Join the club, Stanton. I've felt that way about her ever since I met her back at Drum. She's *really* shit about faking things, but she tries anyway—out of duty, I guess."

"Indeed."

Beyond the windows, someone climbed the rock face. They struggled for a time against the unfamiliar pull of the harness and the strange irregular, knobby, and craggy surface of the climbing wall. A few times, they fell, swinging by the suspension of rope and harness. But slowly, steadily, they rose, ever higher, until at last they stood at the apex of the wall, a little dusty and sweaty, by the looks of it, but unconquered.

Only then did I realize there was someone else following in their wake, someone who had come more slowly but had been watching the path of the first.

"If she's come through this much rough terrain as it is," I mused, as much to myself as to Brynn, "then perhaps it will all be all right in the end. I only hope I might be there to meet her at the summit when at last she finishes the arduous climb."

"Climb to glory, they used to say back at Drum. Motto of the Tenth Mountain."

I smiled to myself as the second climber joined the first. "Climb to glory. I like it. I shall remember that."

The thought stuck with me. *Climb to glory.* After all, wasn't there something I had been holding back? Perhaps if Leigh was to be helped free of whatever cloud hung over her, then maybe I should lead the way in that climb and set the example.

It was time to take my own leap of faith. It was time to tell Leigh-the-soldier about the other Leigh Hunter.

It was time to tell her about the girl I'd left behind me.

FOURTEEN

Leigh

It took a little getting used to, at the beginning, being in a relationship for the first time in a good long while. Not in a bad way—not at all. It's just that when you've been alone for a while, you get used to the rhythm of things being a certain way, and then you've got this whole other person to fit into the picture. It's not gonna fit perfectly, even in a healthy and long-lived relationship, and it's necessarily going to be different. It's just that you all need to put in effort; you've got to put in the work to make that fitting together work out.

It was really good at the start, though. NRE—new relationship energy—is heady. It even made my first little while back at my desk in the commission offices almost not suck. It was a rhythm I could get used to: go to work, embrace the suck, then come home to my girlfriend and my cousin bantering, and have dinner or read or do whatever else suited my fancy.

Chloë hit the ground running, too, with the new job at Red Flag, and I got a firsthand view of it. Some days, I'd take her to work; other days, I'd be the one driving her home, since she still hadn't learned to drive yet. It helped me to know she was taking to the new job—well, to any job, period—so well. Vicariously experiencing the newness of it through her eyes made me thankful to have always had the operative assumption that a job more or less of my choice was at least theoretically attainable, the reality of a gendered pay gap notwithstanding.

But the truth about my job, my frustration, and the fact that I couldn't keep that truth from her forever nagged at me, little by little. I couldn't help it; I had an overblown sense of guilt. And after everything I had endured to get to the point where I could transition, I kind of sucked at faking being happy in unhappy situations that involve biting my tongue for long periods of time, let alone forever.

But by gods, I tried. And when I had somebody else to focus on, it was a little easier to deflect and defer confronting something that difficult. There was plenty going on too. So for a little while, I forgot.

Did Chloë notice? Yeah, I'm pretty sure she did, though I don't know if she knew quite what she was looking at for a while. Even back then, she was good at reading me, regardless of my insistence to the contrary. That knowing smirk of hers, the squint, the glimmer of understanding. I can still hear it: *Lying doesn't become you, darling girl.* But she left it alone, and I was content to leave the matter alone too.

Then came the night of 1 September. Chloë was in high spirits when I picked her up from work, looking tired and happy all at once.

"Hey, babe!" I smiled. "Ain't you a sight for sore eyes!"

She chuckled and slipped off her messenger bag, laying it at her feet as she arranged herself in the front passenger seat.

"How was the traffic?" she asked, buckling herself in with practiced ease. "Not too troublesome coming out of the city, I trust?"

"Mostly painless. Had to take a shortcut to avoid the Market Street rush traffic." We kissed. "How'd the job treat you today?"

"A lot of it was unloading and inventorying boxes, but I also had my first day of range instruction, with Brynn keeping an eye on me for the first little while to make sure I was keeping to modern standards, as taught. There were some reenactors who portray a Union unit who came in wanting instruction on Sharps carbines."

We crested the rise out of the lot and turned onto Route 3.

"How're you handling it, being around old standard-issue equipment?"

"I think I managed all right. Brynn understands that I will not teach anyone wanting to playact as Rebs. I must say, though, I worry about the day someone brings in a Smith. Don't know if I could handle that. Little too close to home just yet." She clenched and unclenched fingers still dimly scarred from all that time ago.

"Been a while since I touched an M24 myself. I get it."

"You do," she murmured, eyes distant as we sped eastward on West Chester Pike. "You do."

The sky was mostly clear that day, and the air was warm but not terribly humid. The tall green trees that lined the road down into Manoa, past the ramps for the Blue Route, gently swayed in the hint of a breeze coming up from the south.

There was a long silence. That wasn't weird, but the silence felt heavy. Maybe it was the work of my anxiety-prone trauma-survivor brain, but I felt like I could hear silences that were *too* long. Like when they were weighted down by the presence of things unsaid.

We crested the rise through Manoa and up into Havertown, and my mental gears started to spin—and the wall behind which I kept things sealed, however awkwardly, started to split.

"Leigh."

I damn near exhaled hard and long enough to blow the car backward. *Fuck. Just in the nick of time.*

Slowly, my heart rate settled back down. After we crested the final rise, the Center City skyscrapers finally resolved into view in the distance, tall and hazy in the late-afternoon sky.

How many times had we followed this road together, up and down, in all that time?

"Yeah?"

"Something's been on my mind, and I wonder if I—if I may have your thoughts on it. I wonder if you've thought similarly."

My heart began pounding again.

"Shoot. Or don't."

"Hah. Cleverly put, darling girl." She turned in her seat, chuckling as she shook her head. "I must remember to use that one with Brynn tomorrow."

"I should charge royalties." I chuckled, the nervous edge a little too sharp in my voice. "But, uh, yeah, sure—what's on your mind?"

"Have you not wondered why it is that—as you yourself said—we have taken to each other so quickly, as if we knew each other already?"

I snorted. "Some people would roll their eyes and call us moving-van lesbians."

We were in Upper Darby now. I paused at the traffic light where West Chester Pike merged with Market, just shy of Sixty-Ninth Street.

I heard her breathe deeply, in, then out.

"That's true, I suppose." She laughed. She sounded a little nervous herself. "I've certainly heard enough about it to think we may indeed have fallen into that pattern. But no, no. I don't know that that's what was on my mind when it came to this."

A strange corkscrew of messy emotion shuddered up my spine. My anxiety started to gnaw, gnaw, gnaw.

"I mean, I'll admit it is kinda wild. Like I've said, I feel less like I met you and more like I *found* you." I shook my head. We were off and up Market, threading through the traffic on the uphill through Millbourne, barely a hair's breadth from my old street. "Like . . . like that satisfaction, yeah? Looking for someone all that time and then suddenly the search is over, boom, you're there, ha ha."

She pursed her lips. "Hm."

"Chloë, hon, where is this going? Seriously, just *say* it."

She looked at me, eyes hopeful. We were stopped at Sixty-Third now.

"Leigh, darling girl. You aren't my first, you know."

Now I was laughing. "Babe, please. You aren't *my* first either, and I know we've talked about this."

She sighed, straightened up in her seat, and folded her arms as we hurried up Market.

"Y-yes, yes, of course. Of course." She seemed to be scrambling for words.

"I knew a girl," she finally said. "I met her in Fishtown by chance, during a raid in 1858."

And she said it. She said it all, word for word. She laid it all out, laid her soul bare, and didn't skim over anything. She told me the story of the woman she'd loved and left behind.

She had been a runner for William Still.

She had been short, probably four foot eleven, and bottom heavy.

She had been a redhead who threw a mean punch.

She had read a lot: Wilberforce, Mott, Longfellow, and more.

She had loved roses—what we'd now call old roses—and she had loved strolling through the garden of the estate at Cloughmore.

On their last night together before Chloë left to go to Harrisburg and enlist, she'd cried, and she'd sworn to wait, even if it took a lifetime for Chloë to come home.

She'd written to Chloë faithfully, right up to the end, right up to when Chloë fell through time after the fighting at Gettysburg ended. By mutual agreement, they'd each burned the other's letters, and Chloë had burned the last she'd received on the night before her unit rode into Gettysburg, in the lead-up to the battle.

There was nothing left of her in the belongings with which Chloë had come through the rift in space-time.

"Her name," Chloë concluded as we came down Broad Street past City Hall. "Her name was Leigh Andrea Hunter."

She said it so reverently, so tenderly, and with such emotion tugging at her voice that I almost missed *what* she was saying.

Then it hit me like a gut punch.

"*Fuck*," I hissed, around a long, unsteady breath out. *Fuuuuck.*

I saw. I knew. Where I'd had a blurry afterimage before, I had the damn nearest thing to crystal clarity then. I'm kind of surprised I didn't crash the damn car but rather brought it all the way back to Federal Street safely, pulling in and parking without causing injury to myself, to Chloë, or to anyone around us.

After I parked, we sat together in tense silence for a long, long time. She could barely meet my gaze. I couldn't *stop* looking at her—in recognition, in shock, but that wasn't all.

I remembered the days before my enlistment, arguing with Mom and Dad about why I wanted to join up—coming up with excuse after excuse but knowing, deep, deep inside, that the inescapable truth wasn't the patriotism, the money, or any of that.

I had been looking for someone. And for the first time since then, I could feel—deep in my gut—that I had just ended that search.

That I'd *found* her.

But I wasn't brave just then. I was afraid.

"Wow." I finally managed to force the word out. I was flabbergasted. I was breathless. "I . . . wow. I don't know what to say."

"It's the truth," she declared, looking up, straight into my eyes. The fire—that intense fire of *you can't conquer me* that had won me from the first day—it was there, and it stung more than a little. "Lying doesn't become me, any more than it does you. I need not swear to you, but it is the truth. It's the truth, and I can prove it."

"Hold the fucking phone. *Excuse* me?"

"Surely Cloughmore House survives, or at least its records. We can seek out the truth—seek it out *together*. I tell you, darling girl, there is naught to fear."

I leaned forward into the steering wheel and buried my face in my hands.

"Fuck. *Fuck.*"

After a long time, I gave up on finding words beyond what I had and unbuckled my seat belt. She took the hint and followed me out. We locked up the car and hurried inside.

I tried to come up with something to say, anything. But I couldn't handle the weight of everything she'd just thrown at me, and the more I thought about it, the more my brain picked at it, the clearer it became: this answered a frightening number of things I'd never thought I could answer.

It was neat. Almost *too* neat.

After sitting in awkward silence by the bottom of the stairs for a while, we split: she went to change, and I went to wash my face and try to collect myself, to no avail.

The Army. The roses. The love of books. The work of William Still.

I found her in the kitchen, nervously munching from a box of crackers, when I returned to the ground floor.

"All right," I said. "All right, I'm willing to grant that there was someone by my name who was a hell of a lot like me. I don't know what else I believe. But before you do anything about that, there's something I need *you* to understand."

I pulled out my cell phone, switched it off, and slipped it into the calf of my boot.

"The commission is responsible for what happened to you."

And then *I* told *her* everything. I didn't give a fuck anymore; I broke a dozen NDAs and told a displaced person the truth: The predecessor of the commission caused the temporal rifts by attempting to change the past to better suit American geopolitical ends. It targeted the Boshin War, a seemingly minor conflict not significantly involving the US and, by doing so, tore holes in space-time. The commission was an attempt at obfuscation and damage control.

"Whatever I am, the fact of the matter is, I share in the guilt for what brought you here. What took you away from her. Whoever she was."

She sat transfixed. I'm pretty sure she'd gone pale.

Her voice, when she spoke next, was pained. "Isn't the truth clear to you? Don't you believe me, after everything?"

It was too much. It was all too much, too fast.

"I don't know, Chloë." I sighed. "I don't know what I believe."

FIFTEEN

Chloë

In many things, I am a patient woman—at least, I hope I am. But when I essay to accomplish something and find my way obstructed, I am not so patient. And when I take a leap of faith, as I did that day on the drive home from Broomall, and find that I am not believed—despite all the truth laid out plainly in the light of day—I do not take well to it.

I stayed downstairs for quite a while that night, replaying the interaction in my head. After it all, after everything, after all the days and nights and the travel and intimacy and everything, it had come to this. Not only that, but she had, in return, revealed that the commission for which she still unhappily worked—or so she claimed—was responsible for the rifts that had brought me to this new time and borne me far from the times and people I'd known and called dear.

It was a revelation I had been wholly unprepared to hear in response.

I caught some small measure of sleep—probably the

least I'd seen since I was last with the regiment. In the wee hours, the quiet before sunrise, I found myself somewhere between sleep and wakefulness on the old sofa, facing the TV that flanked a long-inoperable fireplace, listening to the little sounds of the house and the streets beyond.

I had to know. I *had* to know, by my own hand and with my own eyes, what had become of things. Leigh, so abruptly recalcitrant, was not someone from whom I expected any help. And if the commission's actions, long ago though they might be, had brought me here in the first place, I wasn't sure whom I could trust at all, that morning of September 2.

Rounding up my new Army rucksack, I quietly packed clothing and whatever reasonably portable provisions I could gather from the kitchen. With my telephone and wallet pocketed, I began to work my way toward finding answers.

The city had changed, but not entirely, and after this long in modern Philadelphia, I knew my way. An hour and a half later, I walked up a now-asphalted street toward an old, familiar set of gables.

"We meet again, Cloughmore," I said, greeting my birthplace.

It was the same Cloughmore, though with the growth and modernization of the city around it, the grounds had shrunk. I couldn't find any of the old dirt or cobble paths I'd once known.

Most surprising of all, the graveyard was nowhere to be found, though I was certain I'd come the right way.

I frowned. "They must've moved it." I came up the drive into what was now a parking lot for cars. A sign directed the inquisitive caller to the cookhouse, which it seemed was now a museum office.

In the yard, I finally let myself halt, drop my pack, and breathe deeply with my feet in the grass of the home that had born me. The cookhouse, the mansion—it all still stood, magnificent despite its now far greater age. I turned, regarding all that lay before me.

"Roses . . ."

A pang of sadness stabbed at my heart.

No. No, I mustn't. Answers. Answers!

The woman tending the office on my arrival was alone, a kindly, bespectacled, gray-haired woman attired most elegantly for the caretaker of a museum.

"Welcome to Cloughmore House," she said. "Are you here for a tour? Tours are free, but we charge extra for the special exhibits in the visitor's building across the way."

"A tour, if you'd be so kind," I replied, dipping my head in gratitude. "I'm curious to learn what's become of this place."

She raised her eyebrows in silent reply, then offered a warm smile. "My name is June. I'm the assistant curator here. Our docents are in a staff meeting, and in the absence of anybody else on the grounds right now, I'm all yours. Give me a minute, and I'll lock up here and show you around."

"May I leave my rucksack in the corner here?"

"Certainly—under the coat rack is fine."

"Thank you."

We strolled along the timeworn stones that paved the walk, till we stood at the front steps. How many times had I come this way? How many days and nights had I passed this way before I stood here to bid goodbye to my darling girl and go off to war?

"So," June began, "welcome to Cloughmore House. This house was at the center of the estate belonging to the

Stanton family starting in the early eighteenth century, when James Stanton followed William Penn here and became his secretary. This was only the start of Stanton's long and full career, starting as mayor of Philadelphia and culminating in what we'd now call governor of Pennsylvania . . ."

We stepped through into the entry hall. Here, I'd caught word of John Brown's insurrection and spoken to brave Miss Moses, the indomitable fighter for her people's freedom, who had come from Mr. Still to bring word of our task in securing the safety and passage of Brown's surviving comrades.

June narrated her history of my ancestors and this place I'd once known as home. Yet the specters of my own past seemed to linger here, seemed borne on mystic tides of memory, as we wound from one room to another. Here, I had supped with Mother. There, she had brought me when, unannounced, she'd elected to hire me a femme de chambre and brought back into my life the woman who had tumbled into it at the height of my foolishness.

Oh, Leigh.

Some of the furnishings were as I remembered, but many others were not. I recognized my ancestors' stately bookcases but was aghast that so many of them stood empty. It was here that Mother had taught me how to read and from whence I'd found many a classic tome I'd come to treasure: Parker's soaring rhetoric of liberation and universalism. Wilberforce's and Mott's fierce advocacy of abolition. Longfellow's verse and lingering prose.

June's narrative, and indeed the presentation of what had once been my home, was arranged to reflect the life of its founder, my forebear, who'd come from a little town in Midlothian to take up his work as a businessman and politician under the aegis of the great Penn. It was only on the second floor that her narrative thread wound further forward in time, and so abruptly so that I stopped, frozen in my tracks.

"Chloë Stanton Shaw and her maid, a woman named Leigh Hunter, lived in this room after Hannah Stanton's death in 1859. Chloë's not very well known—we don't even have any likenesses of her—but she's a fascinating woman. It's speculated that she may have been some stripe of what's now called queer."

I blushed. Had I indeed been remembered as such by history? Had I merited remembrance?

"Is that so?" I asked, trying my best to keep on what I had heard Hiromi call my "game face."

"That's what we think, given what little documentary evidence survives. We know she tended to buck gender norms of the time and that she knew how to ride and shoot and was chastised often by her mother for wearing breeches. We think she and Leigh were lovers, but so much of their correspondence didn't survive. We can only make educated guesses."

Lesbian, I'd told Leigh and Hiromi, that morning a few months ago. *I'll remember that one. That word is mine.*

"I wonder," I said to June, "what, ah—what she might say if she had access to the language of LGBTQ discourse and identity that the present time so richly enjoys."

I was still blushing. Lying doesn't become me either, but it wasn't a falsehood—I was merely letting sleeping dogs lie. This woman did not need to know who I was, or who I had been.

"Historians don't ask 'what if,' ma'am. That's the realm of fiction authors, much as the topic can make for a good story."

The bedframe. The fireplace with its blue and white

tiles. The bedside table. All were as I remembered. Yet the place was not a home anymore, merely the shell of one, a fossil through which I was breathing memory for but a fleeting instant.

"I'll grant you that, Madam Curator," I replied, dipping my head in acquiescence. "Now, shall we carry on?"

"Yes. Right this way."

There, walking up the creaking old wooden steps of Cloughmore in tanker boots, rather than constricting, chagrining, flimsy shoes as I once had, I listened to June relate the unimaginable.

Leigh, the girl I'd loved and left behind, had stayed true to her word. After my disappearance, of which she had been briefly suspected, she'd given no intimation of my whereabouts and simply contented herself to serve in the role she'd chosen, as caretaker of this place. She'd preserved it to the best of her strength, in the name of my family to the last. And after many years of waiting for me in vain, the book of her life closed.

As my confidence built, I asked one question, then another, further broadening my appreciation of the history to which I had not been party. June seemed, by turns, delighted by my interest and mystified by the familiarity with the place and its people that could only be borne either imperfectly of great and meticulous study or believably from lived experience.

Leigh had remained faithful.

She'd had a hand in leaving Cloughmore in as good a condition as the now century-old museum had received it.

She had continued her work with William Still's family and had donated to the publication of his memoir of work on the Underground Railroad.

She had died in 1893.

We were on the back porch, overlooking the garden, when I asked June the curator the final question that nagged at me.

"Where was she laid to rest?"

The curator frowned. "She was buried in the family graveyard. And I'm afraid that I—"

"There's nothing left," I interjected, rubbing at tired eyes as I sighed in resignation. "Yes, I know. I could not find it at all on my way onto the grounds."

"It's still not clear why it was done or who ordered it," she offered. "All we know is that it was bulldozed by the city without warning in the 1950s, against the wishes of both the staff here and the few surviving heirs of the Stanton family who were still alive at the time."

I huffed out a long, deflating sigh. My head was still spinning from all of this.

"Shame," I muttered. "A shame. My darling girl deserved better."

"It's really quite refreshing to show around someone with your depth of knowledge on such a lesser-known member of the Stanton family," June offered, gently and perhaps a little diplomatically. "I'm curious, what led you to something so comparatively arcane in Philadelphia history?"

I breathed deeply, trying to think before I spoke. I did not want undue attention, but I feared I'd gotten it regardless.

"When one is connected to a history, for better or for worse," I finally said, "one must face it to move forward and build something new."

Slowly, she led the way back to the office. "Ah, you must be a Stanton relative, then."

I laughed. "Something like that, though these days I

am not certain I know what I am or where I'm going. All I know is that I can't trust those whom I thought I could and that I shall have to seek answers myself if I am to have any satisfaction or resolution."

"Well, whatever you're seeking, I do wish you all the luck in finding it." Inside, she gestured to my rucksack. "It seems you came packed for a long trip."

She offered a hand for me to shake, and after a moment's hesitation, I took it and shook it firmly.

"Travel safe, Miss——"

Hefting the bag back over my shoulders, I paused, briefly contemplating a pseudonym before I threw caution to the wind.

"Stanton," I said. "Chloë Parker Stanton. I have a long way to go yet: Harrisburg and Carlisle, perhaps, but Gettysburg for sure. Madam Curator, it has been a pleasure to call upon you." I snapped my heels together and bowed deeply, like the cavalier I once was.

"Thank you for visiting." She bowed in reply, though her expression remained one of quiet amazement.

And so, I marched out into the parking lot. That was the first time I took out my phone and found that everyone—particularly Hiromi and Brynn—was looking for me.

"No," I growled. "Answers. Answers."

After several minutes of fumbling wastefully with one unfamiliar app after another, I called up a map. There were many roads, highways and byways and some railways, that spanned our commonwealth of Pennsylvania. On closer inspection, though, Route 30 caught my eye. It went west from here, meandering slightly and drawing quite close to the Mason-Dixon, until it reached a familiar crossroads.

"Yes. It shall be Gettysburg, then."

Roughly noting the way from here to the nearest point

of Route 30, I squared my shoulders, hefted my rucksack, and started my westward way to and along Route 30, the whizzing cars and high-wheeling red-tailed hawks my only company for most of the journey.

Truth be told, I didn't know what I hoped to do upon my arrival in Gettysburg. I didn't know whether I'd find somewhere to stay, to start over—but then, could I even do that? This era was not the same regarding such things, and I could see, even at the outset, the many ways in which I might yet be tracked, discovered, and brought back, and not necessarily by anyone with my best interests at heart.

Not long after I reached Route 30 and turned west, I got another message from Hiromi.

<fstopcutie>: Where are you? I missed you this morning. Left out fresh muffins, even.
<me>: Leigh has betrayed me. I'm off to seek answers.

I didn't know what kind of answers I sought, but I wanted them. And somehow, I knew I had to go to Gettysburg to find them. For the sake of avoiding interception, I couldn't risk any conveyance but my own legs, and so I went.

It was a leading.

Without my own vehicle and without the means for a ticket to take me and with the Spirit tugging at my heart, it was only right to walk.

I was no stranger to hard campaigning. This would be a challenge, but I'd weathered worse.

I kept my phone pocketed for a long time and tried to ignore it. Occasionally, it would ping or ring. But I had a different purpose now, a different aim, and I couldn't let anything, or anyone, sway me from achieving it. On and on I marched, even as cars whizzed and rushed past on the road. The day wore into afternoon, and then the rosy hues of sunset spread like a celestial watercolor across the canvas of the wild horizon.

The city was far behind me, but my surroundings still looked decently suburban. In resignation, I retrieved my phone to check my location and progress. I was still on the outskirts of Philadelphia, by the looks of it, and I needed to find a place to make camp, whatever form that happened to take.

Then I saw a message from Hiromi.

<fstopcutie>: Leigh's being an utter turnip. What happened?
<me>: It's a long story. I'm off trying to figure myself out.

A few moments later:

<fstopcutie>: When are you gonna be back?
<me>: I don't know.

It was the honest truth.

There was a long pause. I was coming up on another small array of shops, the thing I'd heard was now called a strip mall.

Another incoming message:

<fstopcutie>: I don't know what the hell she said to you, but you're not helping either, just fyi.

I clambered up an embankment and stood on cement at the edge of a parking lot.

<me>: I know. I'm sorry, Hiromi.
<me>: I'm going to Gettysburg. I was at Cloughmore this morning. I need answers.

Slowly, gingerly, I sat myself down on that curb, phone cradled in my lap and waited for the next message.

I felt so betrayed. Hurt. I had thought that Leigh of all people would've understood and wouldn't have kept something like that from me. Whoever she was in relation to the girl I'd known all those years ago, I could not ignore that she was party to the organization that had caused my fall through time in the first place. This was a good time in its own right, but I wanted to go home. I wanted to go *home*, and now that was never to be.

<fstopcutie>: Send me your location—you can do that, right?
<me>: Yes.

I keyed the appropriate tab and sent her a map square. I was barely to the edges of greater Philadelphia.

After another few minutes came her reply.

<fstopcutie>: All right. Here's what you're gonna do. You're gonna go up the road another mile. There's a little roadside motel, an inn, that you can check into. You've got your bank card or at least some cash on you, right?
<me>: Not much, but yes. Both.
<fstopcutie>: You're gonna march up there and book yourself a room. You're gonna keep your phone charged. You're gonna message me if you need money. If what you need is to go to Gettysburg, I'm gonna make sure you get there. We can figure out what comes next after that.

There, on the berm of the strip mall parking lot, for the first time in that heavy, difficult day, I cried.

<me>: Thank you. Thank you.

With the motel ahead of me and Gettysburg far beyond to the west, I marched on.

Sixteen

Leigh

In the six years since it happened, I've always hated 2 September. It's my anniversary of fucking things up. And let's be real. I fucked up.

Don't get me wrong. On a purely chemistry level, there was never any doubt—none at all. In all the time Chloë and I had been together since May, it was amazing how good our chemistry had been, seemingly out of nowhere. I'd had no business feeling like I knew anything about her when she'd fallen into my life from out of nowhere. But from the get-go, there was something beyond me—beyond her too—that seemed to recur, like an old refrain from a half-forgotten song.

Little things in shared moments. Pangs of what had to be déjà vu all around town. Over and over and over, this happened.

Inasmuch as my gut-level attraction to her was beyond question, after that revelation on the drive home, everything else got to really be too much for me to handle without feeling majorly spooked.

Then it had all tumbled out. I refused to believe any of what she had said, so I told her everything I'd been holding back.

I felt like shit, but I'd said it all, and I figured that whatever happened, happened.

Besides, she had her job at Red Flag now, and I had my duties to return to. Couldn't that be enough? Couldn't we leave well enough alone?

But while I wasn't looking, Chloë took action where I wouldn't.

She didn't come up to bed by the time I fell asleep that night. That wasn't a big deal; I couldn't think of what more to say, and I figured she couldn't either. Anyway, she kept different hours than I did during the week. When I woke the next morning, she was absent, and I didn't think much of it—again, she kept different hours and had other people who drove her some days.

Mac's quietly worried text message later that morning was the first sign I had that something was up at all.

<vapedyke>: *Your gal didn't turn up to work. Every-thing okay?*

Like I said, I had no clue that anything was amiss.

<me>: *We had a bit of a fight last night, and I haven't heard anything from her since then.*
<vapedyke>: *Wait, hang on. 'A bit of a fight'?*
<me>: *Had to do with my work and some unresolved stuff from before, for her. She just . . . I dunno.*
<vapedyke>: *Do you have *any* idea where she is?*

The growing corkscrew of anxiety was back again, twisting in the pit of my stomach.

<me>: *No.*

It sucked, but one thing I've never done is lied to Mac. When she replied, it was three simple words.

<vapedyke>: Then find her.

So I tried. I pinged Chloë, who by now had a smartphone and was at least a little practiced in using it.

<me>: Where are you? Mac is messaging me.

One minute passed, then another, and another.
There was no reply.
Be that as it may, I still needed to get to work by eleven that morning. As I showered and then waited for the coffeepot to chime, I tried to think of where to look. I thought back over what had been said, but I couldn't think of where to begin. I was dressed, breakfasted, and heading to the car before it occurred to me to check with Hiromi.

<me>: Have you heard from Chloë? Mac says she didn't show up to work today, and I can't find her.

A long pause.

<fstopcutie>: Yeah. Yeah, I did.

"Come on, keep moving. Come on." I had to urge myself on, despite an urge to freeze in horror. I was in the car when I got Hiromi's next message.

<fstopcutie>: What did you *say* to her.

What could I say to that? I couldn't very well tell Hiromi what I'd turned my phone off to say in the first place.
So I told her what I'd told Mac.

<me>: My work and some unresolved stuff from before, for her. She just . . . I dunno.

Start the car, pull out, don't think about anything but the road.
My phone dinged and dinged and dinged as I crossed
Broad and headed west. It wasn't until I turned north
toward Stanton Square that I hazarded a glance.

> *<fstopcutie>: Uso tsukanaide. Don't lie to me.*
> *<fstopcutie>: Whatever you said, it's gonna take more
> than 'I dunno' to make it right.*
> *<fstopcutie>: This isn't some army or govt shit. This is a
> woman's heart.*
> *<fstopcutie>: You know better than this.*

I didn't say anything more. I didn't know what to say.
I had to get to work, and I had to focus on the thousand
and one priorities that that entailed from the moment I
crossed the security checkpoint. So I set my phone to "do
not disturb" and tried to focus on work—tried to get into
the headspace of the stone-cold, hard-charging soldier I
used to be.

It lasted until about lunchtime. It was uncomfortable,
really uncomfortable, to pretend to be the hard charger
anymore—obviously, because I'd still been in the closet
when I was a soldier—but beyond that, I just couldn't get
away from everything and be all business and detachment.
The root of what had happened with Chloë, the cause of it
all—I was in it and I was part of it. I couldn't escape it.

Hiromi wasn't going to tell me anything. Mac didn't
know anything. What else did I have? Who else could I turn
to, to figure this out?

I soldiered on. That day and the next day and the next.
My interactions with Hiromi were cordial enough but
tense; if she was in touch with Chloë, she was obviously
unwilling to tell me anything. Mac and I exchanged messages daily—but with nothing new to tell her about the

whereabouts of her newest employee, there wasn't much I could tell her that she didn't already know.

There's a word in Japanese: *gaman*. Stubborn endurance in the face of impossible and trying circumstances. So I put on my best *gaman* face and tried to hang on.

It wasn't until the morning of the fifth day that I reached my breaking point.

Hiromi was again out of the house by the time I woke up and hadn't messaged me in the interim. I tried to carry on as usual, but it felt so hollow. I made it to work early, just like I used to, but I only made it as far as the parking lot. I pulled in and turned off the engine.

I thought I was ready to get inside and get back to my desk and to my work. But for the life of me, I couldn't move. I couldn't make myself unbuckle my seat belt, get out, lock the car, and go into work. I was frozen, trapped under the weight of everything, and even just being there *ached*.

I don't remember how long I sat there, transfixed, the memories of everything replaying in my head. Every time I thought back to something Chloë had said or done, it hurt worse. And the things I'd felt—that I'd seen, heard, and remembered—regardless of what the truth of them was, they had happened too. Could I just ignore them and pretend they didn't exist?

Could I pretend I'd never met Chloë?

I thought back to that day in July at Wissahickon Park. That quiet, clear thought that had seemed to spur me on.

I'd follow you anywhere.

Could I really live without that, having seen what I'd seen? And if I did manage to find her again, would she even forgive me?

Could I keep working in this place, which had given

me direction for a while and was a secure job, but which my conscience clearly detested?

Could I carry on being at odds with Hiromi and leaving Mac worried and waiting when both felt so deeply wrong?

I'd follow you anywhere.

The words drifted through my mind, clear and sharp and unmistakable. The sight of Chloë, confident and in her element in the paddock at the Langley Stables flashed through my memory. Hadn't that been the first time I'd dared even think those words?

I'd follow you anywhere. It had seemed so effortless then. It had seemed so natural.

After a while, I noticed I was crying, but I also noticed something else. I felt scared, but at the same time, through the fear threaded a thin, little edge of clarity that seemed to slowly grow.

I thought of that morning around the breakfast table, with my ancestor's bow behind me and the weight of all that had been unsaid weighing on me. Chloë's words had been simple and direct.

What if you do justice to your ancestor's legacy?

Eventually, it was like somebody hit a light switch. I dried my eyes, pulled up my email client, and quickly tapped out a message to my supervisor.

Dear Martha:

This message's purpose is twofold. First, a personal emergency has come up that requires my attention, and I will not be coming into work for the next forty-eight hours while I address it. Second, this is to state, for the record, that I am giving my two weeks' notice, at which time I will resign from federal service to pursue other opportunities. I trust that you'll forward this message to the appropriate author-ities in preparation for my departure from the JTIC.

Service with you has been an honor.

Very respectfully,
     Leigh A. Hunter

The words were out; they were there on the screen: I'd said them. They were out.

I muttered a hurried prayer.

"*Namu Suwa Daimyojin.*"

My finger didn't even hover over *Send*. I mashed it, *hard*, and then I was off. I was out the gate and onto the street just a couple of minutes later, tears still in my eyes, but that thread of clarity growing into a wave. There was no taking it back now; I had only one way to go, and that was forward.

I'd follow you anywhere.

I called up my phone's virtual assistant.

"Orihime, is there a museum in Philadelphia called Cloughmore House?"

Through the car speakers, Orihime replied.

"Best transit time by car to Cloughmore House, Germantown: fifteen minutes."

"Plot a set of directions and navigate."

I'd follow you anywhere.

The thought still rattled around my mind as I rounded Swann Fountain and turned northwest on Ben Franklin Parkway, bound up for Germantown. Fear rose in my gut, but that current of calm, of clarity, carried me ever on. It was time to face everything from which I'd been so futilely running.

Within minutes, I came up the street to the broad, grassy grounds that ringed the old mansion, the remnants of the once-massive estate that had belonged to Cloughmore House and the Stantons of Germantown. My heart was in my throat, right up until I pulled the car into a parking space by the mansion and swung open the door.

How to explain it? How to explain what I felt at Cloughmore?

Have you ever heard the expression "someone is walking over my grave"? A strange, all-too-familiar chill that you can't quite place, can't quite put into words?

It was like what I'd felt before—like that day we came up Delhi and I saw the strange house on the end of the row by Bainbridge. Familiarity where there shouldn't have been any. But layered over that was something else. Something stronger, deeper. Willing one foot in front of the other, I hurried up the old flagstone path and under the arch, in the direction of the sign that said HOUSE TOURS THIS WAY.

The green grass lawn that lay between the long outbuilding and the main house glistened in the morning sun. Sparrows chirped in the nearby trees. Something I saw out of the corner of my eye seemed to grab me, and I turned, even before I knew what I was looking at, my feet carried as if by something beyond me. The grass gave way to dirt and a little path that wound among the bushes.

"Old roses," I gasped out in recognition. And though I was hearing my voice, I felt as though someone else spoke through me. "Mrs. Shaw's mother planted these."

"That's right," came a friendly woman's voice from behind me, across the grassy courtyard. "Welcome to Cloughmore House—have you been here before, then?"

I turned to find a gray-haired, bespectacled woman, who looked to be about my mother's age, coming out of the outbuilding that had to be the museum's head office.

"I don't . . . know." My words came out halting, unsure. Again, I felt like I was coming unmoored from the here and now. "I don't know."

The woman pursed her lips, then smiled and shook her head. "No worries. We'll be glad to give you a tour all the same. I'm June, the assistant curator. If you'll step this way, I'll find one of the docents."

I was soon met by a short, energetic person in a buttoned shirt and bowtie, who wasted no time in ushering me around to the front of the house. Their name was Riley, and they were a graduate student at Penn, acting as docent here as part of the work for their degree.

"So welcome to Cloughmore House. This house was at the center of the estate belonging to the Stanton family starting in the early eighteenth century, when James Stanton followed William Penn here and became his secretary and, later, mayor of Philadelphia . . ."

Stepping into the brick-paved vestibule left me in awe. It was a magnificent interior, and it still carried the grandeur that wouldn't have been out of place in the home of any wealthy Pennsylvanian family of that kind of long standing. I followed Riley along from room to room, hanging on their words, a little giddy inside but unable and unwilling to look away. This was it; this was the thing I'd been afraid of.

The tour, and the current layout of the house as a museum, was focused pretty strongly on the eras of James Stanton and, to a lesser extent, his grandson, the globe-trotting doctor turned Pennsylvania senator, George Stanton. It was relevant, yes, and it was important, yes, but it was a century too early for anything I was looking for.

But the second floor—the corner room overlooking the garden—that's where they finally said it.

"Much later, George's great-granddaughter, Chloë Stanton Shaw, lived here until her disappearance in 1862. She's one of the Stantons who are lesser known, but the curators tell me that, occasionally, we get a Philly queer history nerd who comes through and asks about her."

The room. The bed. The shuttered windows.

"What do they say about her?" I asked, my voice reedy, breaking.

"Well, we want to be careful about putting words in the mouths of historical figures 'cause modern terminology didn't exist back then," Riley cautioned, looking past me to the blue and white porcelain tiles lining the fireplace. "But they say she might've identified as some stripe of LGBTQ if she were around today."

I had to stifle a laugh. *Yeah, no kidding.*

"What happened to her?" I asked, trying my best to keep my tone steadier than my emotions.

The air in the room felt heavy with memory. It was the feeling you might get when you walk into a place where you used to live—it was home once, and the walls and windows and maybe some of the furniture are still there—but it's different. It might hang heavy with the shades of what used to be, but it wouldn't be *home* anymore.

"She and her mother lived here after the rest of the Stantons moved to other newer houses around greater Philadelphia. She had some involvement with the local abolitionist movement—that much we know—but the details are sketchy. She probably burned anything we'd now count as records since abolitionist work, particularly directly with the Underground Railroad, was still technically illegal at the time. Then in 1862, she vanished. Nobody really knows why. There was a search, but she was never found."

I bit my lip. *Fuck. Fuck, fuck, shit, fuck, damn.*

"Wow. That's a . . . that's a shame."

"Yeah." Riley nodded, frowning. They turned to lead the way out of the room and back into the stairwell. "It's really quite tragic. Though what's interesting is that her personal maid—who was briefly suspected in Chloë's disappearance—wound up being one of the longest-lived caretakers of Cloughmore. A lot of the good state of the museum as the foundation received it was because of her work."

I blushed hard and tried my best to follow close beside Riley.

"No, ah . . . no kidding?"

"Yes. She lived pretty quietly, from the looks of it. Was particularly fond of caring for the—"

"Roses," we said in unison.

Riley turned, eyebrows rising in curiosity. "You're familiar with her?"

How was I *supposed* to answer?

"Lucky guess, I suppose," was my hurried, muttered reply.

We wound our way up and then all the way back down, winding up in the flower garden. I kind of dissociated my way through the latter half of the tour. Like I said, the place hung thick with what I had to admit, even at the time, *had* to be memory.

There was no other way to explain it. I was standing in the ghost of what used to be. Yet here were the roses, growing anyway, blooming anyway, still beautiful. Still sublime.

Riley led me back to the outbuilding, and the museum office, where we'd begun our tour.

"Her name." I'd been so absorbed, I'd forgotten what

I'd meant to ask from the beginning. "The woman—the caretaker. Do you remember her name, by any chance?"

"Hunter," the tour guide said, wrinkling their nose in momentary contemplation. "Yeah, I think that was her surname. Not sure, though—"

"Yeah, that's it," June, the assistant curator, chimed in from where she sat with a stack of papers. "Leigh Hunter. Lived here through her death in 1893. She was buried in the family graveyard."

I tried my best to keep my composure, but I'm pretty sure I was visibly going pale just then.

"Where's that?"

The curator frowned. "Nothing's left of it. City government bulldozed it outta nowhere without telling anyone in the fifties." She gestured out the open door. "Used to be just next to the current eastern edge of the park."

"Wha . . . what's there now?"

She sighed and shook her head. "The local stretch of Sixteenth Street."

"Fuck," I rasped. "Fuck. *Shit*." My head was spinning. I felt like I'd been punched in the gut.

"You're not the first to ask about her," June offered, rising from her seat. "There was a woman who implied she was a time-displaced Stanton here several days ago. I showed her around myself."

"Oh, hey, I heard about her!" Riley chimed in. "Kinda bummed I didn't get to see her in person. Sounds like that was an interesting time. Do you think she was the real deal?"

"I don't know. She seemed to be, in how she spoke and the details she was familiar with, but she was wearing digital camo and a leather jacket and had an Army rucksack. Said she was on her way out of town. Didn't look like anyone we've got photo evidence of. But she sure seemed to know a lot about Leigh and about one Stanton in particular—"

I drew in a sharp, pained gasp. "Chloë!"

The curator turned sharply, shock clearly written on her face.

"Did she say anything more?" I asked, the tension audible in my words. "Did she tell you where she was going?"

June spoke haltingly. "Who . . . is she? Is she . . . missing?"

"Should we contact the police?" Riley asked, trying to be helpful but clearly without anything earth-shatteringly new to offer.

"I've been trying to find her for days. I need to find her. I need to—"

"Oh, oh, yes. She did say something about continuing on west."

A charge of shock went through me. "Please tell me she said where she was going!"

It took me a moment to realize that in my haste, I'd gotten close enough to the curator that I was towering over her, and she rightfully looked a bit flummoxed. I took a step back, eyes averted, briefly chastened.

"Sorry, I just . . . this is really important. I need to make this right."

"She mentioned Harrisburg, Carlisle—oh, yes, of course, and Gettysburg."

Panic momentarily stabbed at my heart.

I need to make this right, I reminded myself. *I need to make this right.*

"Can I get your name, in case she contacts us?"

It was no trouble to dig up a business card from my wallet. But as I began to hand it over, I remembered: *I resigned this morning.* I reached for the pen on the worktable, scratched out everything but my name, and substituted my personal email and cell number instead.

June accepted the card, squinted at my handwriting, and then looked at me as if she'd seen a ghost. Where I would've freaked out before, I only found myself laughing a little, in relief and acquiescence.

I guess I am a ghost.

"Call me if you hear anything from or about her," I urged, dipping my head in a bow of acknowledgment. "And thank you. *Thank you.* This means so much to me."

I raced out the door, out into the parking lot, and soon had the Subaru in gear, over the river, and hurtling north and west up Interstate 76. I must've been speeding at least a little, but it was the furthest thing from my mind.

I was free. I knew what I had to do.

"Orihime, call Hiromi Mitsuya."

"Calling."

The phone rang and rang and rang without end.

"Hi, you've reached the voice mail of Hiromi Mitsuya. Leave your message and phone number after the tone, and I'll get back to you as soon as I can."

"*Atashi da.*" ⟨It's me.⟩ Then, in English, "Look, I know you're pissed, but I resigned this morning, and I just got out of Cloughmore, up in Germantown. Chloë was there a few days ago and headed for central PA. I'm driving there now. Whether or not you help me is your call. But I'm going, and I'm gonna find her, even if it's the last thing I do."

I punched off the call, growled in frustration, and kept my eyes sharp on the road as I rounded the Conshohocken Curve.

"King of Prussia's about twenty minutes if the traffic's good. Gettysburg's another two hours, maybe. If I haul ass and don't stop for anything, I might be able to shave some time off that."

It was different now. Before, I hadn't been able to see the forest for the trees and hadn't realized how my own indecision was closing off options.

Now? This was familiar territory. Crisis was an old friend. I knew how to deal with crisis—it was strangely familiar, comforting even, and I had clarity there.

Get to King of Prussia, get on the highway, get off the highway, get to Gettysburg. That was the mission. It didn't enter my mind that Chloë might not have been there at all, nor did I care whether my cousin called me back. Right then, getting across the state was all that mattered. I could figure it out along the way as I went. At least then, maybe I could live with my conscience.

My phone rang.

"Call from Martha Stavridis," Orihime announced.

"Ignore it," I ordered.

Through the chaos of the big interchange at King of Prussia, I wove my way up the on ramp and merged into the lines of cars heading for the gates. The system read my car's toll tag, the gate went up, and I was off.

So. She'd been right. She'd been right, and I hadn't even had the nerve to entertain the notion that maybe, just maybe, I was the one who was wrong—that I was the one who needed to take the bigger leap of faith.

"She might not want to see me even if I did track her down," I thought aloud. "She'd be in her right to send me away too. She poured her heart out, and not only did I not believe her, I'm guilty by association. I'm party to the organization responsible for bringing her here in the first place."

"Call from Hiromi Mitsuya," Orihime announced.

"PUT IT THROUGH!" I yelled and then winced at the volume of my voice, a little too loud.

"Hey."

"I just got on the turnpike a little while ago. Talk to me."

There was a brief pause. I heard her rearrange herself in what sounded like her office chair.

"So, you finally decided to make things right."

"Yeah. Yeah, I did. I dunno entirely what I'm doing, but I'd like to think I'm doing the right thing. I'm a little scared, but I resigned a couple hours ago, and if my life falls apart again, I'm at least doing it with a clean conscience." I clenched my fingers more tightly around the steering wheel. *"Kore made no koto, mou kore ijou taerarenai."* ⟨I can't handle more of how things were 'til now.⟩

Silence.

"And for that matter, Hiromi, I owe you an apology too. I'm sorry I let my stubbornness get in the way of doing the thing I should've done all along."

She sighed. "I've been talking to her ever since she left, but I think she runs out of battery power here and there, so I'm not in contact right now."

"Where do you think she's headed?"

A pause.

"Gettysburg. She's heading for Gettysburg. I think she should be there by now, but I'm not sure."

That was the first major bit of good news I'd had all morning.

"I expect I'll be there in a little over two hours. Message me if you hear more from her."

"I will."

Far to the west lay Gettysburg and a chance to set things right.

SEVENTEEN

Chloë

On September 7, after five days on that long, solitary road from Passyunk Square and Germantown, I arrived at last in Gettysburg. With Hiromi checking in with me daily as time and my phone's battery power allowed, I had found housing every night, rough and modest though it tended to be—at least it wasn't outdoors.

It was a decidedly less gallant entry than my first arrival there on that late June day, but a strange peace came over me as I marched up the final stretch of Route 30 into town from the east. I'd set out thinking to also visit Harrisburg and Carlisle, yes, but after the first day, I'd thought better of it. It was not those places that drew me, after all. It was not those places that would have the perspective and answers I sought.

The town I found before me was rather bewildering in its extent of unfamiliar familiarity. It echoed the Gettysburg I'd seen, and it was clearly a town alive, but it was a modern town that wore the trappings of its nineteenth-century finery over everything. Where Philadelphia had kept

the best of its old self but woven it—sometimes unskill-
fully—through the tapestry of its present appearance, Gettysburg had visibly made July 1863 its identity. Yet from all
I had observed on the road, perhaps it was fortunate in that
regard. There were small towns that had little more than
one traffic light, a gas station, and one dilapidated clap-
board house after another. In embracing the memory of
that American Armageddon, perhaps the little crossroads
of Adams County had saved itself.

After that first restless night, I had found the old
rhythms and habits slowly returning along the course of my
long, solitary march. This was familiar territory to me—familiar roughness—and it was often familiar terrain as well.
I may have been footsore upon the conclusion of my journey, but I had that strange peace and clarity spreading over
my heart.

"I did it," I said to those old familiar streets. "I'm
here."

I picked at the remnants of stale potato chips and foul
public fountain water as I marched farther into town.
Ample signage and a few municipal maps guided my way
from there, out of the town diamond and down south to
the ridge where much of the battle had been fought after
the first day.

The little stone wall was still there. This, I was told by
the signage, was something called the Bloody Angle, where
on the third day—while my regiment refitted and rested at
Westminster—the Rebs came clear across the open field
and were cut to shreds.

But for the presence of the tourists who'd come to see
it, it was quiet. But the quiet was strange—a deep and
heavy quiet, one that seemed to hang thick with the weight
of all that had happened on that ground. In its own way, it

was funny; I was a living ghost, standing there and feeling haunted.

"Leigh should see this," I said to the tall grass beside Cushing's battery. Then I bit my tongue and tried to clear my head of any further thoughts along those lines. After all, what was done was done, and there was no use in further mucking about in my tangled feelings on the matter. She'd made her choice, and I'd made mine.

I looked around at the old cannons, the stone markers, and the Copse of Trees, but they all kept standing their silent vigil. If there was any answer to be found, it was for me to seek and put into words.

With the earth soft and the grass damp beneath my tired feet, I heaved a quiet sigh of farewell and wandered on. I had so many questions about the battle, and now here I was. I would not have them all answered, I knew, but perhaps I could have enough, at least for a beginning. Maybe once I did, then I could carry on with whatever kind of life awaited me in this new era.

After a while, I found myself at a burial ground ringed by a stately wrought-iron fence and tall verdant trees.

"Gettysburg National Cemetery," I read aloud as I passed within its gates. A stately obelisk stood as the focus, with the gravestones standing in neat grey rows that formed a semicircle around it. Some bore marks of past offerings of flowers or flags, while others were devoid of any visible token of a recent visit. With my breath held, I walked among them, among the graves of these people who were once comrades in arms, whom I had known at the peak of life in the nation's hour of need. Some stones were standing, while others were more modest affairs that lay flush with the grass.

A twig broke beneath my feet, and I happened to look

down—straight at a stone that stopped me cold. I think I exclaimed for the shock of it. I had to read it twice to be sure of what I saw. But yes, there it was.

The weathered letters read:

Wallace Caldwell Simmons
Pennsylvania
Captain, USV, 1st Troop Philadelphia City Cavalry
17th Pennsylvania Vol. Cavalry
Civil War—Spanish–American War
September 12, 1833
December 2, 1901

Once I'd collected myself, I knelt and laid my hand reverently atop the letters that were all that remained of the man who'd been my teacher.

"It seems I found you at last, comrade," I murmured to his aging stone. "I'm late, but at long last, I am here."

It took me a moment to realize that there was more to the inscription. With a carefully placed brushing of the thumb, I swept back caked mud and bits of grass.

Medal of Honor, read the inscription's final line. I gasped.

So many people of this time, particularly Americans, are so strange. They seem to worship the ground a hero walks upon—but then they will turn and curse them as though they were a traitor the moment it's revealed they are queer, they are brown or black, or they are an immigrant or something else. As if the heroism had never occurred to begin with!

For all these decades, Caldwell had lain in hallowed honor here. What would such people today say, were they to learn that he and Nate had been what is now called trans?

Though by the same token, what would *trans* people today say?

People like Eun-seok.

People like Leigh.

I was sure there was no more hope for any kind of progress from her—she'd made up her mind on the course she wanted to take, after all, and would not be moved. Yet I wanted so much to bring her here, to show her this grave. To tell her that people like her had always existed—that they numbered among some of the bravest souls I had ever known, in war and in peace alike.

"I shall write about you, Caldwell," I declared to my comrade's ghost. "I shall remember. We must always remember."

I had to keep moving then. Darkness would fall soon, and I needed to seek some small measure of sustenance, to say nothing of needing to find a place to rest my tired bones for the evening. I rose, shouldered my pack, and walked on through the silent field of memory, through the last bivouac of my long-lost comrades of the old Army of the Potomac.

North, north, back up the Taneytown Road, my boots beat the old route step on warm asphalt, back into a town that still amazed me with how familiar, yet changed, it was. Many of the buildings looked exactly as I recalled, even if there were new structures, electric wires, blacktop roads, and everything else of the modern age crammed in, between, and around them. The town clung to its past as Philadelphia had, though in a different way.

I stopped at a little coffee shop off the town diamond. I had seen much, and my thoughts weighed heavy. I needed to stop, and the cool, airy interior was a welcome oasis.

"Hey, welcome to Susannah's. What can I get ya?"

The clerk working the counter had me smiling despite myself, and then I realized why. Perhaps it was the undercut that offset thick hair in graded purple tones, or perhaps it was the russet tones of a familiar flag pin worn on her lapel. Beneath a tartan blouse hanging unbuttoned was a t-shirt bearing the words *GETTYSBURG UNIVERSITY*. Something about her seemed familiar, but I couldn't quite place it.

Still, I breathed more easily—and it meant something, to enter the establishment of another lesbian, and a black woman at that, who was quietly and openly going on with life in a Gettysburg peaceful and free.

Again, I thought of Leigh. What would she say, were she here with me?

"Americano, please," I said, placing my order. "And do make it a medium, if you'd be so kind. The road has been long, and I have much farther to go."

"Comin' right up." She set to work on the machinery behind the counter. "You look like you've been on the road awhile. Visiting from out of town, I take it?"

It took a moment for me to come to my senses.

"Hm? Oh, ah, yes, I suppose that's the case. Came from Philadelphia."

"That's a nice long drive, but the Turnpike's hella expensive."

I shrugged. "Even longer of a walk on Route 30."

Amid her cleaning of the steaming coffee machine, she gasped, then whistled in amazement.

"Holy shit, forgive me for being blunt, but no wonder you look like you've been roughing it. You still got a ways to go?"

"Yes—I mean, no. I mean, well, there was a girl . . . I

don't know where I'm going. I don't know what I'm doing, but I can't go back. So I thought to come here, where it began, and maybe some sign would show itself—maybe I will yet learn where to go." I frowned and shook my head. The fatigue *had* gotten to me. "No, no, forgive me. I shouldn't let my words get away with me like this—"

"Hey." She leaned across the counter and pressed the warm ceramic mug into my hands. "*Honey.* 'There was a girl' is serious business. You should sit awhile and take a load off." She was smiling slightly, her tone hushed, conspiratorial. "My name's Annette, and luckily for you, I recognize another queer girl when I see one."

I was stunned—and happily so, for the first time in a while.

"My name's Chloë. It's nice to be recognized, but what gave it away?"

"C'mon. You walked all the way from Philadelphia—that's what, a good one hundred and twenty-some miles?—because of a girl. Honey, if that's not the most lesbian thing I've ever heard, I dunno what is. Besides, you sound like an uptimer, too, and we've gotta look out for each other in the big, bad twenty-first."

So she was not just a lesbian but a displaced person as well!

When I reached for my back pocket, Annette waved me off.

"No, no," she muttered. "I got this one. Go siddown and take a load off. Take your time. You need anything, you just say the word, all right? I'll come check on you later."

"Most kind of you to do so," I replied sheepishly. "Thanks."

I made for a corner—the one beside the front window. With an outlet in arm's reach and nobody sitting anywhere nearby, it felt perfect. I dropped my rucksack, sank into the comforting softness of the waiting couch, and closed my eyes. It was good to sit somewhere warm and soft after four days like this.

At last, I sat up, plugged my phone into the wall, and set it on the couch's arm to power up and waited. It would be a while before I could use it, but I was in no hurry. After all, hadn't I arrived? I wasn't going anywhere, at least not immediately. Now that I'd come all the way here, I had to figure out the answer to an inescapable question.

Now what?

The couch was soft, my back hurt more than I thought it did, and somehow, before I knew it, I was waking up from fitful dreams, still sitting with my arms folded, and my myriad little aches had somewhat subsided. Beside me, still trailing its long charging cable, my phone waited dormant, recovering charge to its battery. At the bar, Annette sat atop a stool, reading an old paperback. From what I could see from my vantage point, there was not a single other soul in the café.

"Hiromi will be worried. I should inform her of my arrival."

In the gathering dark of the town diamond beyond the café window, the phone screen's soft glow—proclaiming *Charging 70%*—seemed brighter. A pang of anxiety stabbed at my heart. Did I really want to deal with whatever frantic messages awaited?

"Hiromi will be worried," I repeated, willing my heart past the worry. "I should *inform her* of my arrival. It is the correct thing to do."

With a deep breath and a jab of my thumb on the power button, I switched the phone on. My heart pounded in my ears.

"You all right over there?" Annette called.

"I've been putting off getting in touch with someone who's worried about me," I answered.

"The girl?"

I shook my head. "Another girl, a friend. The girl's cousin. She'd been teaching me how to be a photographer. She'll be worried about me."

Annette cocked her head. "So where *is* that girl of yours?"

"Back at her government job, and I . . ."

I tried to think of how to explain it. *She's back at her government job and also buried under Sixteenth Street outside Cloughmore, and her employer is the reason I'm even here, and—*

Then I simply shook my head. "Long story. She needs to decide where her plans and desires lie for the future."

Annette set her book down on the counter and chuckled. "Downtimers do tend to have their priorities backward, don't they? They don't tend to have the kind of drive I've seen uptimers show constantly." She slipped an item out of the display case, then rounded the counter. "Mind if I come sit with you?"

"I'd welcome the company." I gestured to the empty couch facing mine. "If you don't mind my saying, you seem strangely familiar. Almost like I'd seen you before I fell through time."

She set a little plate down on the table between us, stacked with slices of some sort of brown bread. I leaned in and sniffed.

"Banana bread. Better to give it to someone who

could benefit from a little sustenance than to just throw it to the birds or into my composting pile."

I broke a piece off and chewed pensively. Banana was something to which I was still growing accustomed—hardly something I'd known before. But the sugar, and the soft texture, was heavenly after so many days of bare subsistence.

"Now, I dunno if we've crossed paths." Annette smiled. "You might've, if you were from around here or passed through during the battle."

I started. "What did you say?"

"I came from the day of the battle. My wife and I were together when we were thrown forward in time. That was . . . my, over fifteen years ago now, I reckon."

"You were a baker!" I exclaimed, sitting upright. Then I reined in my enthusiasm, sheepish over my outburst.

She squinted and leaned closer to scrutinize me. "Oh lord, don't tell me, you were a *soldier?*"

"Yes—yes, I was with the old Seventeenth of Pennsylvania, in the Army of the Potomac. We were here with the First Cavalry Division; we arrived the day before the battle. You brought out the first fresh bread we'd seen in weeks!"

I sat up and looked out the window at the town diamond, trying to remember my directions. "There." I pointed in what I thought was the right way. "Out beyond the college, on the Mummasburg Road. I—we talked. You didn't stay. Looking for someone, wasn't it?"

"My, my—you're still new in the twenty-first, you remember it all so clearly!" She laughed and sat back, nodding in reminiscence. "Yes, that—that must've been me. I can't remember you—but I remember the cavalry coming in and the campfires down beyond the college. And I was waiting for Susannah. Found her the same day, and not a moment too soon."

"Did you find her before the battle?"

"Like I said, we came through together. First day of the battle. We've been inseparable since we were young 'uns, and I'm glad it stuck through whatever got us wound up here. When marriage equality became law five years back, we got married. Tried to make a go of settling down in New York—that's where I got my degree—but it didn't quite suit us, so we wound up coming back.

"The county's not the same, sure, but I think we're doing pretty good making a life here, regardless. She wanted to be where we started and rebuild the bakery. I found a job teaching at Gettysburg U—with how the teaching business is these days, apparently I'm lucky to have found a stable college teaching job at all, let alone here." She shook her head and rolled her eyes. "But somehow, we make it work. I help out around the café, and here we are. Getting by."

"Well, it is a pleasure to make your acquaintance again, *Professor*." I dipped my head in respect. "And to enjoy the pleasure of your generous hospitality for a second time."

My phone pinged, and pinged, and pinged, with a day's worth of notifications backed up, finally coming through.

"How's the new gadgetry treating you?" Annette asked, gesturing to my chirping and pinging phone.

"It's taken some getting used to, but I'm starting to get the hang of their use. Phones I can handle. Things like vending machines and coffee makers sometimes seem to get angry at me, for lack of a better phrase."

The pinging stopped, and with breath held, I took the phone in hand to check my notifications.

From Hiromi:

<fstopcutie>: You in Gettysburg yet?
<fstopcutie>: Sent you another $50. Don't skimp on eating today like you did yesterday.
<fstopcutie>: Call me.
<fstopcutie>: Seriously. Call me.
<fstopcutie>: Hope you're safe. Leigh is trying to find you. Call me.

Then, from Leigh:

<rosajaponica>: I'm sorry.

Two little words. Two little words that rendered me speechless.

"Everything all right?" Annette asked.

"I . . . it's the, ah . . . it's the girl," I stammered. "It's the girl."

Another ping.

<rosajaponica>: I'm almost in Gettysburg. Hiromi says you're there today. Learned a lot today. I can't unsay what I said. Let me at least apologize. I want to make this right.
<rosajaponica>: Please.

"She wants to apologize. What do I do?"

"I have to ask. Is she an uptimer?"

I shook my head. "Yes—no—it's complicated, and it doesn't make any sense—"

"Chloë, listen to me." She sat up and leaned forward to offer a hand, which I took gladly, grateful for human contact after five days. She squeezed my fingers. "Breathe, honey. Breathe. That's it. Breathe."

I groaned. "I don't know what to do."

It was the truth. I'd had plenty of time over the preceding five days to try and work through things, and I couldn't quite figure out how to untie that particular Gordian knot.

If she was still so steadfast as to stay in her position, there was nothing to be done. If she was unwilling to hear me when I told her the truth as I saw it, then there was nothing to be done. And with my being here at all, in this land of hybrids and jet engines and smartphones, there was definitely nothing to be done.

"What do I even say to her?"

"You and I have gotten a second chance at building a life. You want my advice? You shouldn't waste that chance. If the girl wants to come apologize, let her come apologize." She squeezed my fingers again and then let go, sitting back. "Life is too short."

I took a deep breath, thumbed through my messaging options, and with a lingering sense of dread, sent my location.

I sighed, buried my face in my hands, and tried to collect my thoughts. I shall ever be grateful that Annette sat with me, letting the silence stand for a time.

"What do I even say," I finally murmured, softer this time.

"You listen," my benefactor instructed. "That's all."

Out of the corner of my eye, I saw someone come into view on the sidewalk beyond the window.

"Hey." Annette gestured. "That her? Looks like your girl made it."

Those colorful tattoos, peeking out from beneath that leather jacket and pretty dress. I heard myself gasp.

"Go, go on," my benefactor urged. "*Go get her.*"

I rose, transfixed, and abandoning everything at my

seat, flew out the door to meet Leigh out on the sidewalk. The traffic rushing past us through the town diamond had dropped to a murmur, and the town's ambient sounds— music from a nearby tavern, the murmur of the night breeze, and hints of distant conversation—were all far more distinct.

She paused, a bit beyond arm's reach, wide-eyed.

"I found you," she sobbed out. "Oh gods, finally, I *found* you. Two lifetimes and I finally *found* you."

I think that was when I made my peace with it at last—knowing that she, too, understood. Yes, of course, Leigh-the-soldier was not precisely the same woman as the Leigh I had left behind on that sad October night in Germantown. Yet life changes all of us, and who shall say that I myself am the same person who rode from Cloughmore House that long-ago night to spirit myself to Harrisburg and into the Union's service?

She was not the same one, and yet she was, brought back to me by fate's wind. She was the same tune played on a new instrument.

"You came." I took a step closer, gazing up at her in amazement. "You came for me, darling girl. You came after all."

"I said I'd explain, and I want to explain everything. Then I promise I'll go away if you never want to speak to me again. I visited Cloughmore this morning and asked around. Everything seemed so weirdly familiar, and I . . . I finally understand."

There were tears in her eyes, and her voice trembled. "I'm scared, but I think I finally understand. Looking for someone all those years in the Army as if they were there and I just had to find them. Why I chose South Philly. The Still house. The memories of roses. Cloughmore. This isn't our first time. All this time. It was all from before, the same patterns, the same rhythms. And it was *you*!"

My mouth was agape. I wasn't sure how to reply.

Finally, I cocked my head. "What of your job?"

"Today. I handed in my resignation before I started on my way here. I don't know what to do next, and I can't change what was done all those years ago, but it's within my means to cut loose and move on with my life somewhere else.

"So seriously, Chloë, if you never want to have anything to do with me ever again, you'd have every right." She wiped a hand over her eyes as her tears flowed freely. "But I couldn't live with things being as they were before, either way. Ultimately, I'm done being miserable, and you shouldn't abandon Philadelphia and a new life at the start of everything just on my account. I can't change what was done ages ago, but I wanted to make it right, so I had to come tell you in person that I'm taking a stand, here and now. I'm unfucking what I can save. You've been nothing but kind and honest with me, and I'm sorry for everything, but most of all for being such a clueless fuckwit and not trusting you. And I, I—"

Something came over me then like a wave. I flung myself at her, arms enfolding her and holding tight.

Deep inside, I felt such relief to be there. To be where I belonged.

"Oh, my dear darling girl. Do not urge me to leave you or to go back. I will go where you go, and I will stay wherever you stay. Your people will be my people, and your God my God."

"I don't understand—"

I found myself weeping for joy and relief as I explained.

"That means I love you, Leigh," I declared. "It means I love you and I'm yours! I want you if you want me, and I never want to be apart from you again."

Her arms closed around me, and she laughed around her tears.

"I love you too, Chloë," she murmured. "For the good days, the bad days, and all the days between."

High above the town diamond, the stars were coming out, as if in recognition and joyous celebration. Far to the east of us, beyond the Susquehanna and the Schuylkill, lay Passyunk Square in South Philadelphia and the chance to come home at long last.

Yet there in her arms again, after all those years, after all those battles, after all those miles, I finally understood.

I was home already.

EPILOGUE

Leigh

So that's our story. That's the long and the short of how we did it: how Chloë and I began to come to terms with our mountain of unresolved baggage from this life and the last and, in the end, despite it all, still chose each other.

That wasn't our last time in Gettysburg—not by a long shot. But in hindsight, I guess it was our first time as a couple.

You may well ask if I remember any more of the nineteenth century than I did at the beginning. Did I learn any more about that other me? How did I come to grips with the fact that I'm alive yet there's a whole other me who lived before—an abolitionist firebrand who's dead and buried and whose bones rest under the asphalt of Sixteenth Street in Germantown?

Oh, *honey*. That's not the point.

What matters is, from the moment of our reunion outside Susannah's on the Gettysburg town square, Chloë and I always came home to each other. It took some doing to reassure everyone back in Philly when we arrived—and you better believe that my last two weeks on the job as a federal agent were more awkward than the tail end of my Army service. But somehow, it was easier to face those things because we didn't have to face them alone.

For the record, we both now work at Red Flag. Mac still drops the occasional *I told you so* in my direction.

Was it happily ever after? No. But it was hand in hand, facing all of life together: the good days, the bad days, and all the days between.

Just under five years to the day after I took my leap of faith, quit my job, and drove like a maniac across the state to chase after the girl I knew my heart recognized, we returned to Gettysburg for the first time as wife and wife.

It was a couple of months after our wedding when Chloë's first book launched, and the three of us—she and I, and Hiromi as official photographer—did a cross-state book talk tour. It was long; it took us from home in Philly all the way out to Erie, and back again. We kicked off at home in South Philly at the Silver Bullet and a couple of the local bookstores, then stopped at Hiromi's alma mater in Collegeville, spent a week at a few venues in Lancaster, and then visited a museum in Harrisburg before we made it to Gettysburg for her talk at the university.

Look, obviously we made waves when the story came out. A story like ours was going to make waves one way or another—between the queerness, the radical abolitionist politics, and everything else. Did the haters show up? Yeah, they sure as hell did. But so did a hell of a lot of amazing, supportive, and kind people of all stripes, online and in person at these events, to talk and share their own stories or their family stories. Chloë wasn't the only real-live nineteenth-century abolitionist and Civil War soldier around in the twenty-first century—but she was probably the only queer one. And with a story that sat squarely at the meeting point of all those things, it seemed that people were interested in talking.

"Hey, Annette! Susannah! Over here!"

Annette and Susannah have come to be good friends of ours, even if I did meet them under less than dignified circumstances the first night I rolled into Gettysburg five years back. I don't claim to know how people like Chloë and them feel when they've found not just other uptimers but even people they knew from before—not the recycled kind like me. But it seems like it's a blessing all around. Despite differences in background, perspective, and privilege, it seems like they can be understood by each other in a way even I can't.

Knowing what I know about interacting with other veterans and how we speak the same professional language, to a point? I think I understand it, just a little.

We exchanged hugs there in the parking lot outside Masters Hall after the book talk. Chloë was wrapping up, rounding up her things inside with Hiromi's help, and I was rearranging things in the aft section of the Subaru.

"Thank you so much for everything today," I said to Annette. In her role as a professor here, she'd been our faculty sponsor for the day. "I'm hoping it moved some hearts, to hear you *and* Chloë together, talking about the fight here in a way that made people uncomfortable with what they thought they knew."

She breathed deeply, sighed, and nodded slowly. "It's not easy at all, but the story needs telling. History needs a shove sometimes. I'm glad to see y'all putting in the work out there. Maybe some folks will think twice about their assumptions now."

With her arm around her wife's waist, Susannah gave Annette a gentle squeeze. "You did good, baby. You did real good."

"What goes, Leigh?"

Chloë called from down the long walk to the building, hefting the last box of books. Hiromi followed behind, several bags in each hand.

We all rearranged ourselves as they came up and around the back of the car. We fussed over settling the contents for transport, chatting about the talk and the last couple days of our visit here.

"All right, I think we're sorted," Chloë declared, pulling the hatch shut. "Shall we meet at the cemetery, then?"

Annette nodded and waved a hand in salute. "See you there."

After a short drive, we pulled into the lot by the national cemetery. Chloë led the way through the stately gates.

It's funny. A lot of kids who grow up in bigger schools around Pennsylvania have come out here for field trips at an early stage, and I'm sure that, as with most kids, they haven't cared particularly deeply about the significance of the place they're visiting. I'd never been out here until that day I came after Chloë. Now, coming here with a partner and friends who actually remember the war and the battle, I think I can appreciate it in a way I couldn't have if I had come here as a hapless, clueless kid from suburban Philadelphia.

The national cemetery here, just off the battlefield, is sort of what I see in my mind's eye when I imagine an old-school nineteenth-century military cemetery, with the classical statues at the center of a half-circle of gravestones, some standing and some flush with the dirt. This place is famous because Lincoln gave his address here, but for me, it has an immediate significance, one that I soon found myself standing beside in the soft afternoon grass.

The grave was simple and unassuming, a low grey stone flush with the grass. The grass around it had been trimmed back since our last visit, and the words *Medal of Honor* at the bottom were clearly visible where once they'd been obscured. I had never known Caldwell, yet he'd helped Chloë come through the war, so he was important to me too.

Chloë knelt, and I followed. She brushed a hand over the name: *Wallace Caldwell Simmons*.

"Morning, Caldwell. Been a little while since I came by. I've brought an entourage along to see you this time."

There was a pause. Then the briefest hint of a breeze shook out the folds of one of the little pride flags, as if in response.

"A good omen," I said.

Chloë reached out a hand to squeeze my thigh.

"Kondo issho ni kite yokatta." ‹*I'm glad you came with me this time.*›

Chloë's memoir had made Caldwell's grave a point of some attention. It was the first that anybody in the present had learned about Caldwell in any depth, let alone learned that he was trans.

"The grave of a trans man, known, in South Central PA," Hiromi remarked in awe. "Wow, I was expecting it to be defaced, not gonna lie."

"Oh, don't worry." Annette flashed a grin. "We keep an eye on him. Least I can do for a trans brother. I bring some of my students out here at least twice a year and make sure that all's well."

Hiromi was already crouching in the grass a half step behind Chloë, adjusting her DSLR camera's lens and lining up a close-up shot from beside the little flags. She snapped a couple of shots, then rose, brushing the grass from her leggings.

She smiled. "Sounds like he's in good hands." Then, to Chloë: "Have you found Nate's grave yet?"

Chloë shook her head. "Not yet. After 1870, it's like he falls out of the records. I'm hoping to go into the archives in Somerset and dig some through the more local records. It's had to wait a little while, but we'll find him too."

We parted ways at the cemetery—Susannah and Annette for home, and the three of us for our bed and breakfast reservation in Ohiopyle, our brief respite before Pittsburgh, where Chloë would next present at the venerable Carnegie Library. We paused, however, just a stone's throw beyond the college grounds, pulling in under the Eternal Light Peace Memorial for one final visit.

"Watch the road before you cross," Hiromi cautioned as we unbuckled ourselves. Then to me, quietly: "Look after her."

Mummasburg Road was quiet as we crossed on foot onto Buford Avenue, where the monument waited.

The monument is one of the ones that's farthest out from central Gettysburg, there on Mummasburg Road, a mighty pale slab of rock on Buford Avenue that stands practically at the edge of the land belonging to the National Park Service. The bas-relief sculpture shows a cavalry trooper sitting straight in their saddle, carbine at the ready, eyes forever seeking the coming of the Rebs over the next ridge.

This is *her* monument, I know—a commemoration of the Seventeenth Pennsylvania Volunteer Cavalry's role here at the battle that, together with Vicksburg, changed everything during the summer of 1863. The regiment fought on and stayed in through the end of the war in 1865, but this was, arguably, its shining hour.

It's peaceful out there on Mummasburg Road, at the crest of the ridge where Chloë's division began the battle on the first of those three fateful days. Okay, yeah, that's hardly a revolutionary statement; everybody who's been through there says that Gettysburg is peaceful when you're not dealing with crowds and you aren't there on the anniversary. Big deal.

But for me, after surviving battle after battle, it had a different meaning. On an old battlefield that's this quiet and this full of nature, to call it peaceful is anything but idle, empty praise.

No, it *means* something. And with all that as backdrop and preamble, standing at the monument itself has its own meaning. It's all too easy for some to pretend that the people who fought on this road that day, like those everyday heroes who fought slavery in the Philadelphia streets and elsewhere before the war, were as stoic and cold as the monuments that commemorate them. But there are those from the Civil War who arrive in the present—the short way, not like me—and remind us that their contemporaries were real, were flesh and blood, and that we must continue their work of fighting injustice and agitating for equality.

And now I get to share a life with one of them and fight on with her at my side. *Again.*

"I find myself in mind of Melville's closing words," Chloë said.

"Melville—whales, right?"

She looked up at me, chuckled, and shook her head.

"He was, as I recall, quoting from the book of Job. 'I only am escaped alone to tell thee.'"

Chloë gave my hand one last squeeze and then stepped forward, phone in hand with roster waiting. As she stood with her shoulders squared and back straight, I could see something of who she'd been all those decades ago, when she was here.

"Company F!" she called. "Sound off for roll call!"

One by one, Chloë read aloud the names of her comrades from Company F, starting from the company's first commander, Captain Charles Lee. I've learned many of these names and their stories—like Caldwell Simmons and Nate Yoder—over the last few years, and as much as I never knew them, I couldn't help but ache a little on her behalf. Like she says in her book title, Chloë was the last. There were no voices to answer the impromptu roll as we stood in the tall grass on Buford Avenue, beside the Mummasburg Road.

It had to be lonely, being the last.

She finished, pocketed her phone, and bowed at the shoulders toward the monument. But I noticed something she'd missed, and when she turned to look up at me, I shook my head.

"Couldn't help but spot an oversight, wife mine. You forgot one," I quietly observed. "Most important one of all, at least as far as I'm concerned."

"Eh? Who'd I forget?"

"Chloë Parker Stanton."

She started at that—but then understood. With a wistful smile, she sighed, then squared her shoulders. As she faced the monument again, her hand found mine, fingers closing, squeezing tight.

Then she spoke the one word that carried the weight of everything—the good days, the bad days, and all the days between.

"Present."

ILLUSTRATIONS

For quite a few years, I've enjoyed illustrating my work as much as I've enjoyed writing it. It adds further depth to my understanding of characters to do so. I've included a few pieces here to give you a taste of the art I've created while developing *Grey Dawn*.

The following pieces are just a small fraction of the art I've created, thanks to the support of my patrons on Patreon. There's much more *Grey Dawn* content that you can catch up on, including bonus scenes, at www.patreon.com/riversidewings.

Character sheet: Chloë Parker Stanton, ca. 2026.

Character sheet: Leigh Andrea Hunter, ca. 2026.

"Really now? That good?"

"Oh, you're looking hella good."

Leigh and Chloë on the archery range at Suwa Shrine in Wynnefield Heights, Philadelphia, September 2025.

6'0" vs. 5'3": Case in Point

During the initial conversation about the cover, this was a mock-up I drew. Clearly, we went in a different direction!

A moment from work at Red Flag, ca. 2025. Chloë tests a refurbished Spencer carbine. In her right hand, she holds one of the Spencer's cylindrical magazines.

ACRONYMS

CBD: Cannabidiol. An extract from cannabis that can be administered as medication for PTSD.

DD 214: Department of Defense Form 214. A document issued when a service member is discharged from active service.

DFAC: Dining facilities administration center. This an early twenty-first-century term for what used to be called the mess hall during the Second World War.

DSLR: Digital Single-Lens Reflex. A type of camera that allows for interchangeable lenses that can be swapped on and off a digital camera.

ISIS: Islamic State of Iraq and Syria. Also known as Islamic State of Iraq and the Levant (ISIL). A militant group and unrecognized proto-state that claims a large swath of Iraq and Syria.

JTIC: Joint Temporal Integrity Commission.

KATUSA: Korean Augmentation to the United States Army. A branch of the Republic of Korea Army made up of drafted personnel who serve out their enlistment in US units of the Eighth Army, the major American military command in South Korea.

MG: Machine gun

MP: Military police

MRE: Meal, ready to eat. Standard battlefield rations of the Army.

NGB 22: National Guard Bureau Form 22. A document issued when a service member is discharged from National Guard service.

NJP: Nonjudicial punishment. A form of discipline administered to enlisted soldiers that doesn't require court-martial.

OCP: Operational Camouflage Pattern. Sometimes also called Scorpion. The current (as of 2020) camouflage pattern of the Army.

OP: Observation post. A temporary or fixed position from which soldiers can watch enemy movements and coordinate artillery and air support.

PAFA: Pennsylvania Academy of the Fine Arts. An art school in central Philadelphia, founded in 1805. Noted American expatriate painter Mary Cassatt was a famous alumna.

PTSD: Post-traumatic stress disorder.

ROK: Republic of Korea. This is the formal name of South Korea, as opposed to DPRK (Democratic People's Republic of Korea), which is North Korea.

YPJ: Yekîneyên Parastina Jin. An all-female, mostly Kurdish militia fighting ISIS in Syrian Kurdistan.

Want to Learn More about the Real History?

Jazz great Charlie Parker once said, "You've got to learn your instrument. Then, you practice, practice, practice. And then, when you finally get up there on the bandstand, forget all that and just wail."

This applies to many things, including responsibly writing a novel that involves history, even one like *Grey Dawn*, which goes into the realm of urban fantasy. This is not a history book, of course, but a lot of history went into making it. It isn't just history writing that's like this, though: any writing project involves a whole hell of a lot of research, planning, and background work—the proverbial nine-tenths of the iceberg that lies beneath the surface.

It seems to me that it's only right to show my work and give you a list of some of the particularly noteworthy books, websites, and podcasts that were instrumental in crafting this story. Some of these, like Chamberlain's *Passing of the Armies* and Moyer's *History of the Seventeenth Regiment*, are now well inside the public domain and can be conveniently found on Archive.org.

History isn't a parade of dates and facts. If you ask me, it's quite likely the most captivating story out there. Don't be afraid to explore!

And we haven't heard the last of Leigh and Chloë. Keep a vidette line posted. They'll be riding back your way before too terribly long.

Yours in solidarity,
    Nyri

REFERENCES

Books

Bilby, Joseph G. *Small Arms at Gettysburg: Infantry and Cavalry Weapons in America's Greatest Battle.* Yardley, PA: Westholme Publishing, 2008.

Blacker, Carmen. *The Catalpa Bow: A Study of Shamanistic Practices in Japan.* London: Routledge, 1999.

Chamberlain, Joshua Lawrence. *The Passing of the Armies: An Account of the Final Campaign of the Army of the Potomac.* New York: Putnam and Sons, 1915.

Hobsbawm, Eric. *Bandits.* New York: Dell Publishing, 1971.

Hoffer, Peter Charles. *Cry Liberty: The Great Stono River Slave Rebellion of 1739.* New York: Oxford University Press, 2010.

Longacre, Edward G. *The Cavalry at Gettysburg: A Tactical Study of Mounted Operations during the Civil War's Pivotal Campaign, 9 June–14 July 1863.* Lincoln: University of Nebraska Press, 1989.

Moyer, H. P. *History of the Seventeenth Regiment, Pennsylvania Volunteer Cavalry.* Lebanon, PA: Sowers Printing Company, 1911.

Onuma, Hideharu. *Kyudo: The Essence and Practice of Japanese Archery.* Tokyo: Kodansha, 1993.

References

Paradis, James M. *African Americans and the Gettysburg Campaign*. Lanham: Scarecrow Press, 2005.

Pugliese, Patri J. *Pugliese's Dances for the Civil War Ballroom*. Lowell: King Printing, 2011.

Still, William. *The Underground Railroad*. Philadelphia: Porter & Coates, 1871.

Thomas, James E. *The First Day at Gettysburg: A Walking Tour*. Gettysburg: Thomas Publications, 2005.

Will-Weber, Mark. *Muskets and Applejack: Spirits, Soldiers, and the Civil War*. Washington, D.C.: Regnery History, 2017.

Williams, Heather Andrea. *American Slavery: A Very Short Introduction*. New York: Oxford University Press, 2014.

Wittenberg, Eric J. *"The Devil's to Pay": John Buford at Gettysburg*. El Dorado Hills: Savas Beatie, 2014.

Podcasts

Civil War 1861–1865: A History Podcast. Accessed May 30, 2020. https://civilwarpodcast.org.

Dobkin, Adin, and Angry Staff Officer. *War Stories*. Accessed May 30, 2020. https://warstories cast.com.

Hitt, Jack, and Chenjerai Kumanyika. *Uncivil*. Accessed May 30, 2020. https://gimletmedia.com/shows /uncivil.

Linzy, Benjamin. *Evoking History Podcast*. Accessed May 30, 2020. https://anchor.fm/evoking-history.

Mahnke, Aaron. *Unobscured, with Aaron Mahnke*. Accessed May 30, 2020. https://history unobscured.com.

United States Naval Academy History Museum. *Preble Hall.* Accessed May 30, 2020. https://naval -history-lyceum.simplecast.com.

Wisecarver, Trae. *Outlaw History Podcast.* Accessed May 30, 2020. https://anchor.fm/outlawhistorian.

Websites

11th Ohio Volunteer Cavalry (Youtube). Accessed May 30, 2020. https://www.youtube.com /channel/UCezbVOElhYe2hifloUHxypA.

Temple University Libraries. "William Still: An African American Abolitionist." Accessed May 30, 2020. http://stillfamily.library.temple.edu/exhibits /show/william-still.

United States Department of the Interior. National Park Service Soldiers and Sailors Database. Accessed May 30, 2020. https://www.nps.gov /civilwar/soldiers-and-sailors-database.htm.

Bibliography

Califia, Patrick. *Macho Sluts*. Boston: Alyson Publications, 1988.

Douglass, Frederick. *The North Star*, April 7, 1849. Archived by the US Library of Congress. Accessed June 14, 2020. https://www.loc.gov/exhibits/treasures/tr22a.html#obj46.

Garnet, Henry Highland. "An Address to the Slaves of the United States of America." August 16, 1848. Archived by the University of Nebraska–Lincoln Digital Commons. Accessed June 14, 2020. https://digitalcommons.unl.edu/cgi/viewcontent.cgi?article=1007&context=etas.

Longfellow, Henry Wadsworth. *Kavanagh: A Tale*. Boston: Ticknor, Reed, and Fields, 1849. Archived by University of Virginia Library. Accessed June 14, 2020. http://xtf.lib.virginia.edu/xtf/view?docId=2005_Q4_1/uvaBook/tei/eaf261.xml;brand=default;.

Melville, Herman. *Moby-Dick; or, The Whale*. New York: Harper & Brothers, 1851. Archived by Gutenberg.org. Accessed June 15, 2020. http://www.gutenberg.org/ebooks/2701.

Mott, Lucretia. "Remarks delivered at the 24th annual meeting of the Pennsylvania Anti-Slavery Society,

October 25–26, 1860." *National Anti-Slavery Standard*, November 3, 1860. Archived by Quaker.org. Accessed June 14, 2020. https://quaker.org/legacy/mott /no-passivist.html.

Moyer, H. P. *History of the Seventeenth Regiment, Pennsylvania Volunteer Cavalry*. Lebanon, PA: Sowers Printing Company, 1911. Archived by Archive.org. Accessed June 14, 2020. https://archive.org/details /cu31924087985507.

Poe, Edgar Allan. "Annabel Lee." *New-York Tribune*, October 9, 1849, 2. Archived by the US Library of Congress. Accessed June 14, 2020. https://chronicling america.loc.gov/lccn/sn83030213/1849-10-09/ed-1 /seq-2.

Poinsett, Joel R. *Cavalry Tactics*. Philadelphia: J. B. Lippincott, 1862. Archived by HathiTrust. Accessed June 14, 2020. https://catalog.hathitrust.org/Record /002613185.

"The Book of Ruth." *Open English Bible*. Licensed under CC0. Accessed June 14, 2020. https://openenglish bible.org/oeb/2020.1/read/b008.html.

Wikimedia Foundation. "Charlie Parker." *Wikiquote*. Last edited September 26, 2019. https://en.wikiquote.org /wiki/Charlie_Parker.

About the Author

Dr. Nyri A. Bakkalian is an Armenian American queer woman by birth and a military historian by training. She is proud to have called both the American and Japanese northeasts her home. She has produced nonfiction, fiction, and photography content for more than a dozen publications, including two newspapers and five anthologies, as well as for Eisner Award–nominated author Magdalene Visaggio's *Kim & Kim*. What's her secret, you ask? Garlic and Turkish coffee (but really, mostly Turkish coffee). Come say hi to her on Twitter, Facebook, and Patreon at riversidewings.

CPSIA information can be obtained
at www.ICGtesting.com
Printed in the USA
LVHW012123260821
696160LV00004B/434

9 781947 012059